Courtesans — Part III

By
Michael Polowetzky

COURTESANS

Part III

Finale

❖

By
Michael Polowetzky

Courtesans, Part 3: Finale.
Copyright © 2021 by Michael Polowetzky.

All rights reserved. No part of this book may be reproduced in any form or by any electronic or mechanical means, including information storage and retrieval systems, without permission in writing from the publisher and author, except by reviewers, who may quote brief passages in a review.

This publication contains the opinions and ideas of its author. It is intended to provide helpful and informative material on the subjects addressed in the publication. The authors and publisher specifically disclaim all responsibility for any liability, loss, or risk, personal or otherwise, which is incurred as a consequence, directly or indirectly, of the use and application of any of the contents of this book.

ISBN: 978-1-63950-012-3   [Paperback Edition]
        978-1-63950-013-0   [eBook Edition]

Printed and bound in The United States of America.

Writers Apex
Gateway Towards Success

8063 MADISON AVE #1252
Indianapolis, IN 46227
+13176596889

www.writersapex.com

I feel the suffering of millions

–Anne Frank

Pensive Ramble

AFTER ESCAPING PRINCE MARKOVSKY'S stylish garden party, Rolande de Montfort first returned home to cream-colored Baroque No. 3 Rue Artemis. If she was yet unsure exactly what to do or where to go next, one thing was clear to her beyond all doubt. "I need to get out of Paris! I need to get out of Paris at once!" Or, more precisely, the girl knew she must escape the enclosed, rarefied, aristocratic social environment in which, until recent weeks, she appeared resigned to live forever confined.

"I realize now that my destiny is not located holding a powerful man's arm," wrote Rolande to her mother in a note before leaving. *"Where is my destiny found instead? I'm not at all sure. However, I will know where it is once I get there."*

"I know this letter must sound a bit addled, Mama," her daughter admitted. *"Maybe experiences like this make even the best of us addled!"*

"I'll contact you again," daughter further promised, *"when I've at last arrived where I'm supposed to be and finally become what destiny wants me to be."*

"Don't fear *Missy*," whispered Celine after reading her child's letter. "I support you, Sweetheart. Go! Follow Countess Manon's example. Be heroic like Countess Manon! Take up the challenge like my Brigadier! Succeed, and you will become the greatest Montfort Lady of them all!"

I

Over the following eventful period, Rolande traveled the country. Despite many offers of assistance from both Auntie Philippine and Auntie Léonie, along with chivalric Brigadier Aslan's repeated suggestions he accompanies her, Mama's "best genes and *DNA.*" I strenuously prefer to journey alone.

"I am not a *Fragile Female,*" she insisted. "Nor am I a *Damsel in Distress.*"

This expedition took the youthful pathfinder down frequent winding-roads, along seeming-countless serpentine footpaths, through many an unforeseen-byway. Rolande traveled either by train, bus, or, on occasion, by foot. For someone whose intimate contact with France aside from trips to isolated vacation spots had been restricted to Paris and its immediate environs, this trip was one of marvelous discovery, unforgettable, eye-opening adventure. Many of the noted sites–beautiful old chateaus; leaping medieval cathedrals; famous battlefields; mournful, thought-provoking castles–previously known to her only from books and photographs, were now at last brought directly before this pair of so inquisitive, speculative young feminine gaze.

In meandering, round-about motion, *Missy* traveled to Chartres, Vézelay, Sens, Poitou, Angouleme, Troyes, Amiens, Chenonceau, Rheims, Bordeaux, Strasbourg, Laon, Soisson, Beauvais, Mont St. Michel. Next, in a similar twisting fashion, she visited Chambord, Pau, Tours, Caen, Dijon, Bourges, Dijon, Blois, Rouen, Toulouse, Lyon, Avignon, arcassonne, Angers. Many other significant destinations in-between, also encountered the girl's delighted, scholarly investigation.

Increasingly for this young wanderer, her sojourn also possessed an enlightening, revelatory aspect. On each successive occasion, whether she be–contemplating the stunning view from atop some *Gothic* tower; become engulfed in the brilliant multicolored light illuminating a famous stained glass window; or, when she observing ancient Roman aqueducts still bring fresh water to towns and countryside– *Missy* experienced more than just a vivid feeling of current wonder. In addition, the girl received a sensation of longtime-fellowship, of personal belonging! If apparently visiting these sites for the first time, *Missy* was no less aware of the returning to the company of long-cherished friends, boon-companions.

"We're so glad you've come back to us again, Dear!" greeted cathedrals silently.

"How happy we are for you to visit us, once more!" wordless but clear, beckoned the castles to "our sweet little Cherie."

"Delighted we are receiving you yet again, darling!" ancient fortresses and monasteries welcomed the girl in unheard, unmistakable voice.

"And I so much enjoy your gracious companionship too, messieurs, mesdames, milords, miladies!" answered *Missy*, she bowing respectful, curtseying deep, her green eyes teary, demure.

If in books, all the events, places, and individuals associated with them were receded into ages past, each became an actual physical encounter, breathtakingly alive! Quiet, deserted locations of centuries-old history, now changed for this singular girl's special benefit into scenes of the vibrant current action. Heroes and heroines she so enjoyed reading about were transformed into awe-inspiring figures of today!

No surprise then was *Missy* often enlisted by European or North American visitors to introduce them to all the fascinating historic venues left out of traditional group vacations. No accident was she rightfully trusted as a scholar far better equipped to teach extra-curious site-seers about the deeper, more significant aspects of local peoples and their unique story than were official travel guides.

Gladly accepting these requests, she was greatly honored to be asked for her assistance, *Missy* insisted, leading each successive educative jaunt free-of-charge. She was at all times pleased to lead appreciative newcomers through the physical, mental, and spiritual avenues of her own beloved stomping grounds. All these places were dwelling since her earliest recollection amongst this girl's treasured "Medieval-*stuff.*"

II

"It's always so much more exciting–so much more interesting–so much more fun hearing you tell us about the Middle Ages, Mademoiselle de Montfort!" praised Mrs. Jackson, an American lady, as *Missy* led a US mother and her two adolescent daughters through sunny, fecund, snow-capped mountain Provence. This was once a region of painters, architects, pirates, theologians, poets, and troubadours. The latter two celebrated throughout Europe for their beautiful, stirring, poignant, verses.

"Now listen to this one!" advised their young guide in a short pattern dress, white socks, black shoes fastened with a strap at side, and wide white chapeau.

Missy's sweet, mellifluous voice proceeded to sing a famous Twelfth Century refrain. She was reciting the ballad first in the composer's original Langued'oc tongue, next, when the song was translated into modern French, finally, when the verses were interpreted in English.

Her audience clapped long, fervent, the listeners most impressed with the talented girl's artful performance.

Missy cast her green eyes demure, curtseyed deep.

"It's so much fun–especially when you tell us their story–recite us their poems and ballads, Mademoiselle de Montfort!" eager injected daughter Rachel, she wearing a blue baseball jacket, cut-off jeans, white tennis shoes, and *Yankees* cap over long auburn hair. From listening to her guide's colorful account of local culture and hearing its verse, Rachel soon imagined herself too as a princess. She is now the object of all courtly, chivalric love.

"Yes, quite so!" contributed second daughter Amanda. Save for a different given name and contrasting number printed on the back of her baseball jacket, she wore the same outfit as her older sister. "Now wait. Stand still, Mademoiselle Rolande. Smile. Let me take some pictures of you."

Amanda took a series of photographs of *Missy* standing beside a nostalgically ruined castle.

Snap, snap, snap, snap, further camera snap.

"Yes, quite so, Mademoiselle de Montfort!" continued Amanda when she completed her roll of film. "You make all those long-ago events and cultures come alive!–You make them seem as if they exist, are occurring today!–In school, back in the United States, the Middle Ages comes off as so dull, uninteresting, boring, so cut-and-dry–Just a series of dates to try and remember!–When you recount the history, though, when you sing its songs, Mademoiselle de Montfort, those far away times become awesome–*really* awesome!"

"I am sincerely honored, my friends," replied *Missy* addressing her new American chums in *BBC-English*. "The Middle Ages are very special, very dear to me. I hope I might possibly make them dear to you, as well. If I succeed even to just a small degree, that will be more awesome to me than diamonds!"

The songbird again cast her green eyes demure, curtseyed deep.

""Now, please tell us again about the four sisters who became four queens, Mademoiselle de Montfort!" entreated Mrs. Jackson, she, as captivated by Rolande's uniquely insightful accounts and stirring song, as were her two children.

"Yes, yes, Mademoiselle de Montfort!" begged Rachel and Amanda, each sister hugging *our own special Mademoiselle* warmly, each sister fondly stroking *our own sweet Mademoiselle's* long, thick red hair. "Please tell us now, Dear, about Eleanor, Marguerite, Sancha, and Beatrice, the four sisters who became four queens."

"But of course, my friends. I love to tell the tale."

The audience listened entranced.

"Did you know that Cézzanne was also born in this region, my friends?" said *Missy,* after recounting to them the tale of the four famous regal Provencal sisters.

III

"Next, come *this* way," instructed *Missy* on her following jaunt. She is ushering now a much larger number of faithful, attentive followers into a thought-provoking *Romanesque* structure in Poitiers. *Click-click-click-click*–of the teenager's red high heels resonated far in the millennium-old granite edifice."This castle was once likely the childhood home of the most famous 'Eleanor' of them all–Eleanor of Aquitaine. She's also my own personal favorite figure in history."

"And ours as well, Mademoiselle de Montfort!"answered the youngster's many followers loyally, all-as-one. "And ours as well. Mademoiselle de Montfort!"

"This picture *he*re is supposed to be of the great queen, herself!" explained *Missy* wearing a short parakeet blue frock, pointing to the near life-size heroic female figure dominating a colorful Twelfth Century mosaic running the entire length of an extensive left wall. This was a work of art which over nine centuries of dust and grime, war and revolution, vandalism, and willful neglect failed to lessen intrinsic beauty.

At the center of the historical picture, seated atop a rearing white stallion, the mighty queen was portrayed charging fearlessly into battle. With her right gloved-hand gripping the reins, her left raised confidently to heaven, Eleanor of Aquitaine signaled to a host of clearly less-assured male warriors coming up from just behind to follow her majesty's lead into victorious combat.

"Yes, yes, I know exactly what you are thinking," ventured teenage *Missy*, she noticed the surprised expressions on the faces of so many in her camera-snapping, notepad-scratching entourage. "Well, Eleanor was was not a 'Fragile Female.' Nor, was she any 'Damsel-in Distress.' All that–weak, timid, vapid, maiden calling to be rescued from a tower by the handsome hero–nonsense is just a Victorian invention. It's far more likely that in Eleanor's own day, the men were the ones crying to to to be rescued from *her*!

"Is that really what the queen looked like, Mademoiselle de Montfort?" queried one person in the young guide's retinue.

"In truth, we don't know for sure," confessed *Missy*, her long, thick red hair in a pretty face. "No authenticated portraits from that era survive. However, there's no doubt in my mind nor in that of any serious historical scholar or noted art expert that our Eleanor was a real *cutie-pie*–that she was an indisputable *looker*–an instant *show-stopper*!"

She is soon adding: "How do we know that fact to be correct? After all, yearning-lovers, sycophantic-courtiers, needy hangers-on could regularly be depended upon singing their queen's praises to the skies. On the other hand, though–and this, messieurs, mesdames, is the decisive piece of evidence–Eleanor's alluring beauty, it projecting well into her sixties, is no less unanimously confirmed, is testified to, by even all her greatest and fiercest enemies! They, both secular and theological, both Christian and Muslim! Male and female! And we certainly don't normally expect women boiling-over, constantly seething with gut wrenching-jealousy of *La Belle Reine*, to at the same moment often praise Eleanor's 'splendid' looks, to so frequently compliment the queen's 'marvelous' figure!"

"No, indeed, Mademoiselle de Montfort!"

"Now follow me, messieurs, mesdames," advised *Missy*, she next directing her apostles into a throne-room characterized by bubbling marble Cordoba-style water fountains, receding rows of brown and off-white, horseshoe Alhambra-reminiscent columns. "Even after her marriages, first to King Louis VII of France and later to King Henry II of England, Eleanor–in her local Occitan dialect: *Alinor*–still reigned as the independent and quite effective Duchess of Aquitaine. She sat on the throne in this extensive domain. She and she alone issued all the commands here, she and she alone delivered all the instructions, she and she alone received homage–not either of her husbands!"

"Wasn't our Eleanor a noted cultural patroness, too, Mademoiselle de Montfort?"

"You've learned you're lessons well, Madame!" Rolande complimented, the *click-click, click* of her red high heels echoing long and far."Why, in our Eleanor's day, Aquitaine was a great forum of European literary, artistic, musical, even fashion development, display. Aquitaine was a fruitful venue of cultural cross-pollination. The word *chic* may not have existed yet, but our Eleanor was definitely regarded as the chicest of the *chic!* Her duchy was seen as a place only for *chic* people! *Chic* Aquitaine was certainly–***where the action* is**!"

"Why? Back then," giggled *Missy*, "if you were a rube from hillbilly Paris or a yahoo from backwoods London, you didn't know the first thing about the innovative scholarship, about breath-taking new ideas!"In Europe during the Twelfth Century," explained *Missy*, "you didn't know the funniest jokes, didn't know the most intriguing stories or were up on the latest, most stylish fashions until you'd first spent time in culturally-diverse, intellectually open-minded, sophisticated, style-setting Aquitaine!"

Click. Click, click, click–of the scholarly girl's red high heels on granite reverberating long and far.

"Look!" instructed *Missy*, she now directing the viewers' attention to the medieval chamber's seamless blending of two quite separate and distinct schools of art. Here. colorful figurative Christian mosaic historic panoramas coalesced with elaborate, non-figurative, Moorish arabesques to create a single, exquisite, uniform celebration of creative talent. This masterpiece lined all four walls, the ceiling, and much of the marble floor.

"Ooh!" cried the audience in unified admiration.

"In later centuries, men's stupid, icky-politics has tried making us believe that a similar unity is impossible," explained Celine's *Treasure*, she gesturing to the corner where a restoration team's removal of yellowing, chipped plaster revealed that a far larger proportion of the hall was covered by the original multicultural panorama than long assumed. "Luckily, despite the self-promoting office-seekers[2] continued interference, the truth is, at last becoming known!"

IV

"This Dear often sounds and behaves just like Pascale Kedari, don't you think?"

"Yes! So, this sweetheart certainly does!"

"Mademoiselle de Montfort often reminds me of the *Messenger.*"

"This earnest, passionate child definitely reminds me too of our *Messenger!*"

V

"Not much is left of the dwelling today except the outer walls," conceded *Missy* today wearing a soft blue short dress, neutral shade pantyhose, white shoes, and chapeau. She, speaking first in French, then in *BB C*-English, Spanish, German, Italian, Farsi as she led an ever-growing number of diverse-tongued followers around the area once the final home of Christine de Pizan.

"Still, coming to the site is fascinating, Mademoiselle de Montfort!" answered her faithful, camera-snapping, notepad-scratching entourage.

"Notice the walls, Messieurs, mesdames?" said *Missy,* pointing to the moss and wildflower-covered ruins of *Gothic* battlements standing amidst modern cultivated countryside. "Not much else was left standing after the 1789 Revolution. But in our Christine's own time, this place was a quite large, extensive and noteworthy Medieval structure."

"Fascinating Mademoiselle de Montfort!"cried her loyal followers.

Snap, snap, snap additional camera snaps by the girl's studious disciples.

Scratch scratch, scratch, further scratches on their note pads. Further camera-snaps, more diligent scratches on pupils' notepads

"Our Christine was the very first woman in French history–to earn her living entirely as an author," informed *Missy*. "She appears to be the first female professional author in all of European history!"

Snap, snap, snap, camera-snap, Scratch, scratch, loyal note-pad scratch

"Have you got any samples of her work, Mademoiselle de Montfort?"

"Oh yes indeed, messieurs, mesdames! Just one moment."

Removing copies of a *Penguin Classics* paperback from her khaki carry-all bag thrown over her left shoulder, *Missy* proceeded to distribute the copies. "I made sure to bring examples."

"Most impressive, fascinating, beautiful, Mademoiselle de Montfort!" exclaimed her disciples upon setting their cameras and notepads aside to inspect the literature provided.

"This is our Christine's most famous work," instructed *Missy*. "It first appeared in approximately 1405. It's called: *The City of Ladies*. The book still makes awesome, thought-provoking reading even today."

"Ooh!" voiced their guide's expanding retinue, all its members highly impressed, each avidly looking through the pages. "Ooh! Beautiful!"

Written before the invention of the printing press, Christine de Pizan's celebrated book originally appeared as an illuminated manuscript. Some unknown if very talented scribe (quite possibly a nun) filled many of the vellum pages with splendid, multicolored images of queens, female warriors, female philosophers, saints, and scholars were constructing a castle to serve as their own special dwelling, their own sanctuary or place of noble womanly intellectual reflection. This modern version finely reproduced Medieval art.

"The book became very popular," said *Missy*. "Following the invention of the printing press in Germany during the mid-fifteenth century, the *City of Ladies* came out across the continent, published in multiple languages."

"Why did our Christine decide writing it, Mademoiselle de Montfort?"

"Because she became frustrated with the often rampant misogyny of her day, she decided to offer a rebuttal through describing the outstanding women of her culture. Just as Eleanor of Aquitaine was *chic* before 'chic' was invented, so our Christine was a *feminist* before 'feminist' was invented. What was the phrase she wrote? Oh yes, **'Men who slander the opposite sex usually know women who are more clever and virtuous than they.'**"

She then added: "And remember, Christine wrote this in 1405!"

"And what became of all those men who criticized her position, Mademoiselle de Montfort?"

"They are remembered today only for criticizing Christine!"

VI

"So here we are at last, messieurs, mesdames."

"Yes, so here we are, at last, Mademoiselle de Montfort!"

"Awesome is it not, messieurs, mesdames? Really, *awesome*. Even though this city has expanded considerably since the Fifteenth Century, the original positions and fortifications of the medieval armies on that famous morning long ago can still be roughly made out, even today. Awesome! *Really* awesome."

"So they can, commander!"

"Now, hand me my pair of binoculars."

"Hand our commander–Mademoiselle de Montfort–her pair of binoculars!"

Dressed his morning in light khaki shorts, white tennis shoes, a *Yankees* baseball cap, and ivory color pullover sweatshirt with leftist logo, *Missy* and her devoted followers were now atop a grassy, wooded promontory. In the spring of 1429, this area constituted the forward line of the Dauphin's army, hoping to raise the British and Burgundian siege of Orléans. Like scouts reconnoitering enemy defenses without themselves attracting undue attention, Rolande's latter-day troops each lay on their stomach close to the ground.

"See! See! Over ***there*** is where our Jeanne d'Arc ordered the French army to begin its advance" Rolande enlightened her quick multiplying-squad. "See, see! Over *there.*"

After carefully scanning the historic location for several minutes with Brigadier Aslan's pair of military-issue, high-resolution field binoculars, *Missy* handed the valuable instrument on to her nearest aide-de-camp. She also indicated the field glasses were to be shared at regular intervals with all her faithful lieutenants so that everyone present might each obtain a good look at the famous battle site. "See, see, messieurs, mesdames! Over *there*."

"Yes, commander, we can now see where our Jeanne d'Arc ordered the advance!"

"Yes, commander, we can now see where our Jeanne d'Arc started the advance!"

"So we can indeed, commander–Mlle. de Montfort!"

"The Brits and Burgundians were caught completely off-guard by our Jeanne's innovative maneuver," explained *Missy w*ith a wide smile, a deep sense of rightful pride. "Following so many months of bloody, fruitless stalemate, this seventeen-year-old girl–this girl just one year older than me–totally altered the military balance of power in Europe. Within just weeks, she successfully routed the Brits and Burgundians and lifted the siege. She became forever-after– *The Maid of Orléans*."

"And that was only the beginning of our Jeanne's string of brilliant victories!

"So it was, messieurs, mesdames! It was only the beginning."

"None of the old-fogy male generals believed a 'mere' girl had it in, her!"

"No they did not, messieurs, mesdames. But girls can do anything if just putting their mind to it!"

"And while today history, drama, film, fiction, music, painting, architecture celebrate our Jeanne as a great, inspiring leader of men, as a saint, as a national heroine–"

"–the pompous, opinionated male 'experts' are still remembered if at all, messieurs, mesdames, only for being wrong!"

VII

Doesn't Mademoiselle de. Montfort reminds you of the *Messenger* "Yes, the idealistic young Dear certainly resembles our *Messenger.*"

"Indeed, this special child is so similar to our *Little Marie!*"

"Perhaps, she's been chosen to fulfill the martyr's sacred cause?"

"Pray it may be so!"

"Yes, I too, pray it may be so."

"Let us all pray fervently. It's true!"

VIII

Leaping spires
Surging vaults
Running naves
Embracing song
Flooding light
Bursting, glittering rainbow color
Red
Orange
Yellow
Blue
Green
Indigo
Violet

"I finally understand!" cried *Missy*; she becomes one with the spiritual, visual, emotional symphony that is the church built by Blanche of Castile.

"Yes, I finally understand!" again she cried, seeing the words of her summons on the Paris embankment at last fulfilled."Yes, yes! I am yours, and you are mine! I now understand the part I was destined for, and I was born to play!"

Return

Dear Mama,

I am coming home at last! I finally discovered what I was searching for. I hope my decision makes you proud of me. Also, I promise that during my ramble, I did not get into any of what you call "foolishness" or stopped attending Mass. See you in just a few days.

Love, Missy

HER SEARCH AT LAST fulfilled, the young explorer in a sky-blue outfit, chapeau, and heels slipped a postcard through the designated slot in a tall, steel, circular, red, and black mailbox. The words she recorded were penned in a delicate feminine script. On the front side of the postcard was a vivid, colorful photograph of *Romanesque-Gothic* Angers Cathedral in western France. "Mama greatly enjoys receiving periodic notes of a spiritual nature," thought her adventuresome daughter. "Mama will especially like this one."

A further reason was urging *Missy* to at last return to Paris. Inside the beige leather satchel presently slung over her left shoulder was yet another volume the girl unearthed while rummaging through the secondhand bookstalls she investigated in each university or cathedral town. On this occasion, the discovery seemed almost providential. This latest addition to the *Missy Collection* finally made clear the vocation its possessor must now embrace. It was a calling, hinted to her first during the summons on the Right Embankment and later reaffirmed during that transcendent experience in the church built by Blanche of Castile. This was a sacred, unique, lifetime vocation, the new book explained. Rolande must perform not behind the safety of thick, ancient, historic walls but amidst the hectic, violent, uncaring, modern world.

What was this piece of crucial, decisive evidence?

An artist for our time: The Life of Pascale Kedari Castellane
By Sister Claire Preston STM
Introduction by Prof. Matilda-Gisela Eisenberg
Photographs by Sister Genevieve Fauré STM
Raymonde de Charpentier Press

Also, just inside was printed this dedication:

To: Véronique Castellane,
whose kindness and love made this possible

"All of the original *Five Good Ladies* are mentioned!"remarked *Missy* observantly after reading the inscription. "All the original Five Disciples are named!"

Judging by its: tattered, dog-eared condition; frequent underlined text; loosened, creased binding–this biography had already been passed around many times. The name on the title page indicated the volume was printed privately. Today, no regular publishing company, newspaper, or electronic media outlet in France would dare touch this controversial subject. While not formally censored or declared illegal, all public discussion of the Middle Eastern artist was strictly discouraged by all government, education, and cultural authorities. Brought out just a year earlier, this little book looked far older. No wonder it was so cheap!

A jet flew high above.

She, alone in the great wide firmament.

Wanderer looking small and lonely.

Too high to be heard from the earth.

White contrails marked the voyager's course miles distant.

"This reminds me of one of those Soviet era samizdats," commented *Missy* to the Eastern European bookseller as she paid for the volume. "You recall, don't you? One of those works of *subversive literature* by Akhmatova, Mandelstam, Tsetaeva, Yevtushenko, or Solzhenitsyn? Banned by the Communist authorities, these writings were passed around surreptitiously in hastily printed form."

The merchant cast *Missy* a long, suspicious glance. He was a relatively new arrival in the West. The frequent presence of *KGB* officers dressed as unobtrusive civilians, even as schoolgirls, was yet to leave his ready consciousness.

"Are you from Russia, Mademoiselle?"

"No, Monsieur," replied Rolande. "I'm from France." "You enjoy Russian literature, though, Mademoiselle?" "Oh, yes! Very much so, Monsieur!"

She recited aloud verses from the poet Marina Tsvetaeva, in Russian:

> *God placed me all alone*
> *Amid the wide world.*
> *You're no woman but a bird.*
> *Therefore, fly and sing."*

After first looking about to be sure the pair were not being observed by the authorities, the merchant, clearly touched by this chance encounter, smiled at the cerebral youngster fondly, protective. Then, whispering, he volunteered: "The *Messenger*! Yes, indeed, Mademoiselle. Save for your red hair, and you remind of–look just like the *Messenger*."

"Thank you, Monsieur. I'm most honored. I'll do all I can not to disappoint."

Missy was deeply impressed with her murdered fellow adolescent's creative talent. How could she be otherwise?

In Paris alone, great cathedrals, august boulevards, famous plazas, noted monuments, and bridges all continued bearing witness to four-feet-teen-inch Pascale Kedari's brilliant artistry. Her self-taught style was as deceptively simple as it was also timelessly magnificent. Even outside the capital, in provincial cities like Bordeaux, Lyon, Marseille, and Rouen, *Little Giotto's* remarkable frescoes were still present along principal avenues, were yet to be seen within celebrated parks, found on wide church squares.

After the near-successful attempt by her supporters to overturn the reigning corrupt conservative regime, its surviving rump led by President Alexander Markovsky ordered the artist's public works be henceforth denied protection from damage by weather, air pollution, graffiti or other forms of vandalism.

If the bobby socks-Messenger, even in death, was too powerful attacking directly, she might, reasoned her foes, be defeated through the elimination of her memory. Yet no sooner did the government cease protecting these masterpieces than ordinary citizens eagerly took up the responsibility. In so doing, murals first valued for their artistic value became honored too as semi-religious shrines. Growing numbers insisted Pascale Kedari, also called *Little Marie*, was, in fact, a saint.

While she was quite aware of her contemporary's existence, *Missy* never actually met the miniature painter. As a *Montfort Lady,* Celine's daughter belonged to a clan historically committed to preserving the conservative status quo. In contrast, the Middle Easterner, darling of the Opposition, lived under the guardianship of leftist academics, union organizers, avant-garde artists, and social activist nuns. Although once-living just miles apart physically, the two girls dwelt culturally, politically, on different planets.

Still, both the merchant's heartfelt comment and the book *Missy* read with rapt attention as her train sped toward Paris, seemed to confirm that the unacquainted teenagers possessed a critical connection.

Despite the book's tattered condition, many underlined or torn pages, the authors' splendid, poignant words instantly commanded and promptly received loyal attention. The brilliant photographs only furthered the effect. "Awesome!" proclaimed *Missy* as she read furiously on. "No, not awesome, *really* awesome! *Really, really* awesome!"

"I must go and speak to Sister Claire and the other *Five Good Ladie*s when I get back to Paris!" *Missy* pledged. "I must speak to them as soon as I can!"

What precisely she was going to say to people whom she'd never seen before, Rolande was not at all sure.

"However, I do know I must speak to them about something special! It will be something more special than I've ever spoken, ever imagined, even dreamed of mentioning to anyone before! Even to Mama!"

The Red Virgin

"SO, OFF ONCE MORE goes Mama's peripatetic little scholar!" remarked Countess de Montfort. Wearing a short, sleeveless, raspberry red dress, the lady was seated at an open-top grand piano beneath a female ancestor's portrait by Vermeer. During her younger daughter's absence, Celine, too, underwent a life-changing experience. In her parent's case, she was befriending the Iranian-American mathematician Ashraf Kermanshani. "No sooner does Mama's *Treasure* come home than Cherie goes speeding off on yet another expedition!"

"Don't worry, Mama," counseled *Missy*. She was about to exit cream color No. 3 Rue Artemis the morning after her return. "This time, I'll be back in only a few hours."

"Can Mama possibly accompany *Missy* on her favorite Redhead's next extended philosophical campaign?" questioned Celine, her painted fingers dancing across the keyboard, playing Schumann's K*inderszenen*. "We both might each find the jaunt intriguing–we might both discover the mutual effort fulfilling."

"You'd truly like to come along with me, Mama?"

"Yes, *truly*."

"Sure! Sure, you can come along next time, Mama! That will be awesome! No, it will be *really* awesome!"

"Parent and child shall take on the world together."

"So we will!" mused offspring, starry-eyed. "However, first, I must complete my current mission alone."

"Yes, of course, Darling. Mama understands. First, *Missy* must complete her own current mission alone. Just make sure *Treasure* comes home in time for dinner."

"Yes, I promise."

"Wait!" instructed Celine. "First come over to the piano and give Mama a kiss!"

I

"I pledged it was my solemn duty to go and speak to Sister Claire and the other *Five Good Ladies* when I got back to Paris!" whispered *Missy*.

Exiting Baroque, cream color Palais Montfort, the pensive teenager girl advanced through a quiet aristocratic neighborhood with blooming chestnut tree-lined streets. Traffic and urban congestion were nowhere seen or heard. Once again, *The Woman in White,* wore a like-shaded chapeau, short, sleeveless dress; pantyhose and heels.

What precisely *Missy* intended telling Sister Claire and her allies, she was still unsure. "However, I do know I've got to tell them something very special! Something more special than I've ever spoken–ever imagined–ever dreamed of mentioning to anyone–even to Mama!"

Onward, onward, the snappy-clad teenager marched with increasing vigor.

Onward, and just quite possibly *upward* as well!

A new and altogether unique power was visible in *Missy's* stride as she headed boldly toward St. G Church. This nine-hundred-and-fifty-year-old *Romanesque* basilica was situated across town in the 5th Arrondissement. *Missy* often read, heard, and saw pictures of the historic structure. Unfortunately, political events and party affiliations not of this girl's own making long dissuaded her from actually giving the church a visit.

"Well, now I will at last!"

Missy paused, reflective.

"Even me being one of the *Montfort Ladies* won't stop me!"

Not since she was embraced by the spiritual, visual, emotional symphony that is the house of worship created by Blanche of Castile, followed by her seeming-preordained discovery in the secondhand bookstalls outside did *Missy* feet so happy, so elated. Above all, she so confident in making the right decision.

"Mama is going to be so proud of me!

Onward

Onward

Onward, *Missy* advanced with ever-increasing vigor.

Departing the narrow, sinuous streets of the Marais District, she, later, exchanging busy Rue de Rivoli for the Place Hotel de Ville; soon, too, traversing that wide square north to south; finally, crossing the Pont St. Antoine–*Missy*, at last, approached the Left Embankment. In each successive generation or so since well before 1789, large numbers of people collected in this area to register their well-justified dissatisfaction with the contemporary powers-that-be. More often than not, national leaders found no alternative but conceding at least in part to the protestors' demands. "Or if kings, presidents and chieftains did not" added *Missy*, "they soon forever regretting their failure doing so!"

Yet, the girl's ultimate objective was still to be reached.

Advancing next along the riverbank in view of *Gothic* churches and leaping spires, she marching parallel to a mighty medieval fortress and graceful spans across the water, also passing bookstalls with famous, long out-of-print literary works and scholarly treatises– Mademoiselle de Montfort moved ever onward.

Finally, the dainty explorer made a left, another left, a right, then once more advanced straight ahead. This time, she entered the no less narrow, serpentine, Medieval streets of the *Latin Quarter* or 5th Arrondissement.

"Here, I am!" declared *Missy*, at last reaching the front portal of St. G Church, principal meeting-site of the *Five Good Ladies*.

II

Exhausted by the long trek, *Missy* sought to recover her breath, calm her fast-beating heart within the cool, quiet walls of the tangerine, cocoa brown and vermillion-colored *Romanesque* basilica. She was presented alone. Or, so at least it appeared. No service was being performed. No one else could be seen either in the long, vaulted Nave, in the far Chancel, or the adjoining *New Arena Chapel* celebrated for its 64 near-life size murals created by Pascale Kedari.

These pictures, which like those of Giotto in the original fourteenth century Arena Chapel in Padua, Italy, record the life of the Virgin and Christ. Devotional candles set beside statues of saints now reduced to stubs, these tapers were obviously lit by worshiper's hours earlier. After sitting reflective for a time atop a green wooden bench, *Missy* rose to her feet and began circumnavigating the huge, wide, vaulted interior.

Up and down

North to South

East to West

Around again

Click, click, click, click–of teenager's high heels on granite floor resonating far.

Running parallel along the Nave walls, printed on marble tablets each two meters from top to bottom, were inscribed in alphabetical order the names of all the church parishioners who died in *The Great War*. Row after row, after row, after still further row, these lists of the heroic fallen ran. Some were the names of soldiers who died at the First Battle of the Marne, others who gave their lives at Verdun, in Champagne, in Lorraine, at Artois, while scaling Chemin des Dames, also dying at Artois, Cateau, Aisne, at the Second Battle of the Marne. If evoking no immediate personal memories to observers a century following the conflict, each name registered on the wall clearly once belonged to a much loved and cherished father, son, uncle, husband, brother, or boyfriend. The site was deeply moving in its simplistic grandeur.

"I hope the sacrifice of almost an entire generation was not completely in vain," thought *Missy*, no pacifist, as she contemplated the monument. "I hope all those soldiers did not perish for nothing."

"Blessed Virgin," prayed *Missy* softly as she walked around the almost thousand-year-old Nave, "please look after Mama and my sister Ferdinande and Auntie Philippine and Auntie Léonie and Brigadier

Aslan–Please also look after all our loyal servants–and look after the widows and orphans and refugees and displaced people–Please look after Simone Weil, wherever her noble soul now journeys–Please look after Mrs. Jackson and her two daughters and all the other people who asked me to be their guide when I was on my recent travels–And please look after any others I can't presently think of–Yes, please forgive me for not remembering them at the moment. I'm sorry–Also, please give me the strength to say what I'm supposed to say to Sister Claire and the other *Five good Ladies*."

Click, click, click, click–of an approaching second pair of heels reverberated far.

Hello," welcomed the new arrival.

Missy turned around.

"Hello, I'm Sister Claire. Father Richard is currently engaged elsewhere, and he instructed me to take charge."

Echo

Echo

"Is that so?" stammered *Missy* in reply, better words failing.

Sister Claire did not wear a conventional habit. Instead, this fellow redhead was dressed in a light-gray ladies' *power-suit*—wide lapel jacket with padded-shoulders, the hem of skirt above knees, a frilly white blouse with ribbon at the collar, neutral-shade pantyhose, black high heels. Save for a silver crucifix around her slender neck and a wedding-ring symbolizing her eternal marriage to Christ, this lovely lady in her mid-twenties might easily be mistaken for a professor, an attorney, a physician, business executive or any other dynamic young secular career woman.

If this renegade British aristocrat was codenamed by MI6, the CIA, the KGB, Interpol, French, German, Chinese, and Saudi intelligence services as *The Red Virgin,* if her name was included in the *McCarran-Walter Act* list of "subversive aliens" denied visa into the United States, she was also ever-meticulous to appear *proper.* She always sat upright, did not point, use bad language, or put elbows on the table. In addition, she was sure to exit vehicles correctly and keep charming lower limbs crossed. As governess Mrs. Anderson back in England taught her former charge—"A *proper* young lady, the representative of an ancient, historical family, one, who was presented to the Queen, never misbehaves, slouches, eats with her mouth open, or fails to cross her legs!"

She was traveling on a different path than other the girls. In her rarefied, landed-elite, even cynical Paris police readily admitted that "Sister Claire always behaves like a *proper* British lady. She always wears a *proper* dress or a *proper* skirt."

Still, this young lady's illustrious pedigree caused no obstacles to her winning the extensive trust and support among communities far less politically, socially, or economically privileged. After all, were Her Grace the 23rd Duchess of Airandel just ***Slumming-it***, she only **Curious-to-see-how-the-other-half-lives**, or but **Going-through-a-phase**—concluded longshoremen, factory employees, refugees, agricultural workers and trade union organizers, *Milady* would have long since tired of "meeting the peasants" and retreated to the comfort of her own wealthy, titled land-holding origins. As was apparent to all she encountered, *Milady* was made of sterner intellectual, spiritual, if not bodily stuff. Although conservatives like Mama highly disapproved of Sister Claire not wearing traditional women's religious garb, other, less orthodox, more questioning individuals thought her "feminist outfit" made this nun far easier to relate with. Not merely she understanding humanity with the stilted view provided atop a pedestal, Sister Claire, they found a highly approachable and empathetic person. Indeed, to dedicate one's life entirely to God, Sister Claire believed, one must fulfill that vocation not behind convent walls but rather within the world and among the beings God created.

While never diminishing the patrician flavor of her personality, Sister Claire eagerly embraced what she considered her role as a champion of God's downtrodden. Her closest friend and fellow member of their order of nuns, Sister Geneviève Fauré, daughter of a plumber from Rouen, was only the first of many in the European working class wishing to serve as this noble-hearted but physically-vulnerable upper class girl's confidante, guide, and protector.

"I am so glad to meet you at last, Sister Claire," stammered *Missy*. Earlier so confident, she now felt terribly stupid, ignorant, oafish. She wished her cloddish, bumbling, unworthy self might immediately either dissolve in a puff of smoke or quickly be transported to the dark side of the Moon. Inside this medieval church, wearing a short, sleeveless dress, *Missy* became dreadfully cold. She frantically, shame-faced, rubbed her bare arms in search of warmth.

"Here, wear *this*," interceded Sister Claire with a melodic voice. Removing her jacket, she placed it around *Missy*'s shivering shoulders. "You're wearing an adorable outfit today. However, these old, granite churches can often be so cold at times."

"Thank you ever so much, Sister Claire."

Echo

Echo

"I came here today because I wanted to say how much I enjoyed reading the book you wrote about Pascale Kedari," pursued *Missy* as both young ladies settled upon a blue wooden bench. Sister Claire was first studiously crossing her pretty legs, *Missy l*oyal crossing her own, same."The photographs by Sister Genevieve are splendid as well. She's really gifted with a camera! I know of what I speak since Mama is deeply into snapping pictures, too! Has Sister Genevieve ever considered having an exhibition?"

"I am trying my best to persuade her to do so too, but Leopoldine is very shy."

"Maybe Mama can arrange it, Sister Claire? Mama is ever-so skillful at making gifted but shy people come out of –'their shell'– as Mama describes it."

"You might be correct."

"Are the other *Good Ladies* here, too?" ventured *Missy*.

"If you mean Sister Genevieve, Professor Eisenberg, Madame Castellane, and Duchess de Charpentier, no, they are not around. Leopoldine, excuse me–*Sister Genevieve*–is currently returning from Quebec, where she was instructed to open the first chapter of our Order in Canada. Professor Eisenberg is giving a lecture at the Sorbonne. Madame Castellane and Duchess de Charpentier are delivering speeches. However, they will all be back here for Mass on Sunday."

"Should you wish to meet each of them," added Sister Claire, "I am sure they will all be delighted." Although it was actually her second language, the Brit spoke French as though it were her native tongue.

Two pairs of feminine eyes linked.

Sister Claire had a pretty, girlish face with-smooth high forehead and cheekbones; firm chin, fetching green eyes; good, white teeth; straight, sculpted nose; unblemished, palish skin; engaging, welcoming painted lips. Thick, fiery red locks fell below her shoulders, she had a strong, well-developed bust. She conducted herself with a natural nobility of soul, and unaffected graceful, delicate, eager-to-help, deportment.

If a decade older than *Missy*, the nun's years of public advocacy making her far more enlightened than the teenager about politics, social and economic matters, Sister Claire was also a virgin. Her entire knowledge of boys, sex, romance, was restricted to literature, art, the movies.

For a courtesan, this realization was at once both leveling and intimidating. **Leveling**: in that "worldly-wise," *Missy* was the more conventionally "sophisticated" pair. **Intimidating:** in that Sister Claire's un-meddled-with mind and physical innocence signified she dwelt in a far higher, more perfect dimension.

"When I get home, I must take a long bath! And use lots of soap!" thought *Missy*, she suddenly feeling monstrously dirty, wicked, undeserving. "What made me think I ever had any right to enter this great lady's presence?"

Don't fear! I understand! Let's be friends–Sister Claire signaled to her troubled visitor with own compassionate, green eyes. *I want us to become chums, to become special buddies.*

"I am so happy you enjoyed my book," the religious continued in reassuring, confiding, schoolgirl words. "Today, the book is so difficult to obtain. The government does not officially ban it. Still, Markovsky and his cronies make the book very hard to find. Where did you purchase it? Please tell me, and I am most interested."

As the nun crossed her pretty legs opposite, the newcomer loyally followed, same.

"I found it at a secondhand bookstall in Anger, Sister Claire," replied *Missy*, soon feeling at ease. The nun's show of knowing-kindness made the visitor's mounting anxiety evaporate."I've often found such places are the best location to discover fascinating, unforgettable, valuable reading material. Pieces long out-of-print or difficult to obtain normally are often readily available in old bookstalls near marketplaces, along riverbanks, in the squares of cathedral towns. On one occasion, I discovered the first edition of J.S. Mill! On another, the first edition of Feuerbach!"

"Splendid! I must try such an expedition myself." "Indeed, you certainly should, Sister Claire."

*Missy i*ssued a wide, eager, untouched adolescent grin.

She was enthralled to *talk-shop* with a fellow bookworm.

"Don't make yourself a slave to the Internet, Sister Claire! Go and look for yourself! More likely than not, you'll be far more successful finding what you're after in musty old bookstalls than searching o*nline*!"

The pair giggled in mutual schoolgirl-agreement.

Missy paused.

She crossed her pretty legs, opposite.

The hem of her short dress receding.

"You ought to see my growing library at home, Sister Claire. Mama calls it **The Missy Collection**. I started gathering books when I was just four even before my head could reach the top of the merchant's counter! Today, I'm starting to run out of room to place them properly–despite all the new shelves Mama ordered constructed for me."

She is reiterating: "More than a few important books, noted-learned quarterlies and other publications of note, I've unearthed rummaging through old bookstalls. They are usually so cheap, as well! It makes me feel a bit guilty getting them at so low a price–but not *too* guilty! I often think that–"

The Countess's daughter paused, abrupt.

She grew worried

Unsure

Suspicious

Carefully, probing yet with increased certainty, she touched first Sister Claire's face, next, her shoulders, then, the nun's arms, torso, hands, and hair.

"Yes, yes, she's real! She's real!" thought *Missy* with relief. "I'm not crazy. I'm not dreaming! I'm not just imagining. She's not a ghost!– At least I don't think so."

Grown accustomed to provoking such behavior in visitors upon encountering her, the nun made no reaction.

If originally visiting today simply to greet the famous lady, to express her admiration for the renowned Sister Claire, *Missy* now experienced a mysterious, irresistible urge to also embrace the woman. She, to embrace both Sister Claire and the nun's entire dedicated, selfless, committed way of life.

"Whatever 'sophisticated,' 'worldly-wise' advantages I might possess." thought *Missy,* "they are as nothing in comparison to the 'naive,' 'innocent,' 'head-in-the-clouds'-attributes of this particular creature."

The youngster cringed.

Pulled back

Bit her lip

"Don't make a fool of yourself, Marie-Félicitée-Rolande de Montfort!" she scolded herself. "Don't behave like some idiot American rock or movie star fan! Sister Claire will think you're nuts! And she'll be right, too!"

"I so much admire your book, Sister Claire," said *Missy*, hoping her recent enthusiasm went unobserved. "I never truly appreciated, never fully understood the magnitude of Pascale Kedari's art until reading your brilliant book! Reading it changed my life! I really mean it! Yes, indeed! I was long looking for a new direction to take in life, and your beautiful book finally gave me the answer! Your book showed me the path I must take! I know now that–"

Stopping in mid-sentence, *Missy* could not resist once more touching her companion's face; next, she is again feeling her mysterious new buddy's shoulders, torso, hands, and hair.

In time.

Sister Claire now rose to feet.

"I am so honored you enjoy my book," said the Red Virgin, almost apologetic. "I am so delighted the message I sought to convey was appreciated. Since Little Pascale's death, Markovsky's regime has encouraged so much demeaning pop-Freudian drivel, amateur-Shrink babble to be written about her that I felt it was my keen personal responsibility setting the record straight. However–"

"**Rolande**"

"However, **Rolande,** I am just an emissary, an intermediary. Please never forget that! I am merely recounting someone else's story. My biography only exists because our little, exquisite, martyred Pascale first entered the world, first entered my life. The child performed deeds and created monuments worthy of being recorded for all ages to come."

"I seek no personal glory," further insisted Sister Claire. "I wish only to keep Pascale's message alive, work so that her cause may be one day triumph. Triumph not just here in France but across the planet!"

The British nun motioned for the friends to take a walk.

Missy immediately jumped to her feet.

She still clutched Sister Claire's right arm tight with both her own. Just in case this marvelous young lady was, in fact, only a spirit, her admirer was determined not to let this beautiful phantom slip away.

"Come with me, Rolande, sweetheart, "urged the author. "Let me show you something. You've read my account of Pascale's all too short life. You've seen the photos Sister Genevieve took of the Child's brilliant work.Now, it's time you see these frescoes with your own eyes."

Click, click, click, click–of two pairs of high heels in Nave reverberating far.

Sister Claire directed *Missy*, still clutching the nun's arm tight, into a chapel across the way. At this hour, no service was being held there. The cohorts of Japanese gadget-snapping, list-checking tourists, were departed for lunch. Even easily recognizable informers and plain clothes secret police were momentarily gone. The two friends could enjoy the art displayed on all four walls, ceiling, and front altar, alone.

The enclosure 9 meters wide by 40 long, 5 meters high, this celebrated tourist site, Sister Claire explained, was once an unused auditorium with cobwebs, roaches, dust, and chipping plaster. One day, Pascale, she was just recently taken under the *Five Good Ladies'* protection, her gift for painting yet unrevealed, was permitted her request to "fix-up that poor, sad room." When her mentors came for a look several hours later, assuming the girl just scrubbed or whitewashed the walls, they discovered instead, "The Divine Child" was busy at work on a brilliant fresco. Today, 64 of these masterful examples of paint on wet plaster adorned the former half-forgotten facility. Madame Castellane christened the redecorated auditorium "The *New Arena Chapel*" and its shy, four-foot-ten creatrix with jet-black hair always in her face and drooping knee socks, "Little Giotto." The entire world soon heartily agreed.

Without a single day of formal education or art training, she completely self-taught; Pascale's deceptively "primitive" style instantly commands the viewer's rapt, loyal, obedient attention. Her outwardly "naive" manner of portrayal at once makes countless millions aware of the timeless message contained for humanity in each superb picture.

> *–The Valley of Dry Bones; The tyranny of the Romans; Herod and the collaborators; The Annunciation–(you would be scared too if an angel suddenly appeared in your house!); The Virgin's Song of Praise; "For there was no room for them at the Inn;" The star in the East; The Magi; The Nativity; Slaughter of the Innocents; The Flight into Egypt; The carpentry Shop; Mary Magdalene; Christ feeding the Multitude; The Prodigal Son's brother; Christ preventing the Stoning; Christ with the Lepers; The Widow's mite; Christ curing the blind Man; The Good Samaritan; Mary and Martha; Christ raising Lazarus; Christ freeing the woman from the unclean Spirits; The Sermon*

on the Mount; "And Christ Wept;" His entry into Jerusalem; Christ expelling the moneychangers from the Temple; The Last Supper; The Garden of Gethsemane; Christ Betrayed; St. Veronica on the Road of Sorrow; The Crucifixion; The women discovering the empty tomb; "Be not Afraid–

Several images are crafted in bold primary colors: black, white, red, blue, green, yellow; other pictures using more nuanced shades: orange. Aquamarine, violet, camel, burgundy, russet, malachite, amethyst, lavender–these are some of the 64 near-life size frescoes Pascale Kedari renders of the life of the Virgin and Christ. While formally modernized versions of distinctly Christian tales, these works, and the characters, issues, actions they portraydeliver a critical message instantly relevant to persons of every faith (or none at all), to every creed, race, and ethnic group. A vital, nonsectarian, all-inclusive message, which if not for the young artist's tragic death, would at once liberate humanity, overturn this current sorry, materialistic, class-bound world.

"Awesome!" exclaimed *Missy*, at last releasing Sister Claire's arm so that she might study the frescoes closer. "No, *really* awesome!"

"Awesome!" cried the girl, racing about the chapel, she seeming-magically drawn first to one superb picture, then, to a second, a third, yet, fourth. "No, r*eally* Awesome! No. no. *Really, really, really* Awesome!".

"Each of them is so-so beautiful!" she shouted with joy, merrily scampering about from image to image. "Each of them is so-so beautiful! So-so moving! Each fresco is so-so splendid! So-so-so-so marvelous! They're all so Fantastic!"

Contemplating the pictures and the lesson they teach filled *Missy* with a special ecstasy. One, for which there were no words in any of the multiple languages she spoke, to describe. Perhaps adequate words don't exist in any human tongue? This was the same combination of unique joy and sacred obligation *Missy* first experienced on the Embankment! Later, when she was embraced by the sea of primary color that is the church of Blanche of Castile! Above all, receiving this ethereal sensation was similar to Missy's honor upon being granted the privilege to meet Sister Claire.

"The pictures are tremendous!" cried *Missy*. "The pictures are wonderful! Gripping! Entrancing!"

Sister Claire applauded ladylike, offered protective, older sibling approval.

"The pictures are ravishing! Stunning! Radiant! Peerless! Miraculous!"

At last, her teenage heart racing, she exhausted both knowledge of adjectives and oxygen in her adolescent lungs, *Missy* collapsed pleasurably-weary on a green wooden bench. Her white chapeau and purse were fallen several meters away on the granite floor. Thick locks of fiery red hair covered her pretty, girlish face.

"Pascale's frescoes are beautiful, beautiful!"*Missy* gasped in one final effort before she is resting bent over in silence to catch a breath, ease happily bounding heart.

Sister Claire smiled.

"Yes, just as I knew," the nun mused. "She's come at last!"

A moment is elapsing.

Sister Claire pondered

Now, it was the renegade British aristocrat who became determined that if her visitor was but a lithe spirit, a mere fleeting phantom, she not be permitted escaping human grasp.

She held *Missy* tight.

"Ouch!"

Forgive me!" begged Sister Claire, quickly loosening firm grasp. She was both sorry pulling too hard and delighted her companion was not just a supple ghost flown away."Forgive me, Sweetheart!"

"Of course, Sister Claire. Is something troubling you? May I help? Please?"

Tears ran the young nun's cheeks.

Happy, desperately happy tears.

"This is the one!" proclaimed Sister Claire, her voice unconsciously switching into *BBC*-English. "This is the one!–The successor to The Divine Child!"

On a section of the wall just to the left was a fresco of *The Annunciation*. You would be scared too if an angel suddenly appeared in your room! This was one of the several remarkable images found in this chapel where *Little Giotto* both requested and Sister Claire agreed to pose as the picture's main character.

"Don't worry, Pascale" the nun whispered guiltily to the fallen artist as if her beloved drooped socks Pascale was still present. "Don't worry, my special, priceless Divine Child–You, will always be the first in my mind, always the first in my heart, the first in my soul–But now that you're in Heaven–no longer walking the earth–your disciples need someone else to be our formal, public leader, a spokesman–to proclaim your doctrine to the world!–to prove that a terrorist's bullet did not end your story!–To demonstrate that no number of bullets and rockets and missiles and bombs and false promises and tortures and betrayals can ever prevent you, little Pascale, from attaining ultimate victory!"

Teary-eyed, voice choking, Sister Claire now took *Missy* firm by the shoulders and led her up to the fresco. "Sweetheart, you are our cause's new leader!–You are now our cause's champion, our representative to the world!–I saw you possessed this *Calling, Vocation* from almost the moment we first entered the chapel!–Make us all proud of you, Cherie!–Make all humanity proud of you!–Shine out to history!–Let our beloved precious, martyred-Pascale's message, at last,be known, be accepted, revered by all nations and peoples!"

She paused to catch her breath.

"I know you want to it, Sweetheart! I know you *can* do it! I know you *will* do it!"

"I swear to do my best, Sister Claire!" pledged *Missy,* teary-eyed, once more filled with that special ecstasy, that unique combination of joy and sacred obligation she first experienced when summoned on the embankment. "I swear to my best, Sister Claire."

"Fear not, darling. I know, above all, Pascale knows, you *will* be triumphant!"

The pair embraced

Separate souls uniting as one

Time passed

Sister Claire now glanced at her watch.

It was a delicate timepiece on a delicate wrist.

"Mama is likely wondering where her daughter has gotten-off-to," she said, the Brit's words returning seamlessly into French. "Dinner must be approaching. It's best little girls like you go home and eat, get some rest. We don't want Mama getting worried!"

She gave a maternal pat to *Missy's* bottom.

"Now, be off-with-you, dear! I will have plenty of time presenting you to the other ladies on Sunday after Mass?"

III

"What just happened?" speculated Marie-Rolande-Félicitée de Montfort with a worried grimace, the intense emotion of recent event subsiding as the two women near the church's front portal opening onto the serpentine Medieval *Latin Quarter*. "What did I just allow myself to get into?"

"Don't fear," counseled the Red Virgin, she is applying a reassuring peck to her new chum's troubled face. "Don't worry, Cherie! Even the greatest saints suffered from doubt! Even blessed Pascale confessed she harbored misgivings. Remember, dear, we are flawed-mortals, not sinless angels."

"Does she even know who I really am?" thought the young courtesan, still uncertain.

"Yes, of course, I certainly know who you are!" interjected Sister Claire Preston as if reading her companion's mind. She took hold of Rolande's wavering hands, protective. "You are the younger daughter of the famous pianist Countess de Montfort."

The nun is soon adding: "*Our Lady* moves in mysterious ways, does she not!"

On The Wings Of The Morning

YET WHAT OF THE other *Five Good Ladies*–Professor Matilda Eisenberg, Mme. Véronique Castellane, Duchesse Raymonde de Charpentier and Sister Genevieve Fauré? Did they too, judge Rolande as worthy?

In the wake of Pascale Kedari/*Little Marie*'s assassination, the failure of the popular insurrection in her name, and the ensuing electoral muddle, the *Messenger*'s principle guardians would likely be most hesitant entrusting public leadership of her cause to another individual. Especially to an outsider! "Winning the endorsement of the famous Sister Claire Preston, significant as it might be in itself," conjectured Rolande, "is still just the first obstacle I must overcome. In the future, I'll surely confront a far more skeptical audience."

I

For many around the world, next Sunday, Easter, ironically occurring this year on Pascale Kedari's birthday, was the most important day of the year. Although *Missy* originally planned to accompany Mama, Ferdinande (now pregnant), and her husband the Duc d'Aveyron to the family's usual parish, she now prevailed to be allowed to attend the service at St. G Church, instead. Given Celine's increasing interest in "my scholarly *Treasure*'s pensive jaunts" and her recent query if: "Mama might soon participate in one of her child's expeditions," permission was not difficult to obtain.

He has risen.

He is risen, indeed

Clothed all in white from wide chapeau to high heels, from sheer pantyhose to gloves clutching new *Coach* purse, Rolande entered the 950-year-old tangerine, cocoa brown, and vermillion *Romanesque-Gothic* basilica in 5th Arrondissement. Heavy traffic and a jammed *Metro* delayed our heroine's arrival until the service was already begun. Quickly, it was evident that finding a chance to meet or to speak with Madame Castellane and the others would not be easy. Empty saved for Sister Claire when first Rolande visited, today the granite, cross-beamed, vaulted church was now filled with hundreds, more likely, thousands of worshipers.

"Pardon, Madame"

"Pardon, Madame"

"Pardon, Monsieur"

Slide

Slither

Slither

"Pardon, Madame"

"Pardon, Monsieur"

Slide

Slither

Slither

"Pardon Madame"

"Pardon, Madame"

Slowly, forever-ladylike, Rolande navigated through the packed, well-dressed crowd. Many women, like herself, boasted the most impressive headgear. Not only was the Nave occupied long before Rolande entered, but the Chancel as well as east and west Transepts were long claimed. Television equipment set up to record the event additionally hampered any latecomer's way. At last, finding a niche at the rear of a small side chapel, Rolande conceded further progress until the close of service. She sat down upon a green wooden stool, crossed her pretty legs, adjusted the angle of her chapeau and made ready to watch, listen. Every aspect of the ancient, familiar yet on each successive occasion no less memorable ceremony was beautiful. It was as ever a lasting inspiration to the soul, eye, and ear.

Pondering, contemplative time elapsed.

Atop the central, high altar, located at the conjunction of the Nave and Transept (medieval churches are built in the shape of a cross), forty-year-old Father Richard Castellane directed the Mass. He wore a red, white, ermine, and silk cassock elaborately hand-embroidered with cloth-of-gold, enveloping his entire frail body. He also wore cobalt blue alpaca gloves. A large ornately carved ivory Byzantine cross was suspended on his weak chest, a heavy gold chain around his narrow shoulders. Yet further impressive, museum-quality religious chains, emblems, medallions, each crafted by a royal goldsmith now centuries dead, covered the distinguished priest, doctor and archeologists are only just over 100-pound, five-foot-five-inch figure. He appeared so much more robust, powerful, even literally taller than he really was under all that grand imposing attire worn just twice a year.

When he was on visits, trips, outings, at cocktail or dinner parties with intimates, Father Richard dressed in "civilian clothes," in "secular outfits" as his protective, motherly younger blood-sister Mme. Véronique Castellane enjoyed calling "my erudite dear's garb" "my scholarly darling's apparel." This distinguished polymath dressed in a similar manner when performing operations at the neighborhood clinic, delivering lectures on ancient history at the Sorbonne, or while excavating Biblical sites in Israel, Jordan, Turkey, or Iraq. However, given the significance of today's event, the priest so often accused by the traditionalists and parish office crones of being "too-worldly," "too-modern," was seen in his full Easter Sunday regalia.

After Father Richard completed his Homily based on the passage in **John** describing Christ appearing after the Crucifixion first to Mary Magdalene, Sister Genevieve Fauré, also atop the high altar, stepped forward. Rolande offered eager, careful attention. She'd heard much about the lady's excellent singing ability but, unlike her superb photography, was yet to be presented an example.

Rolande wasn't disappointed.

Dressed in a lime-green silk cassock with ornate, hand-sewn gold floral designs, thick auburn hair falling below her shoulders, Sister Genevieve, like Sister Claire aged mid-twenties, performed an unforgettable, personally composed ballad. Her sweet feminine voice echoed beautifully up and around the soaring Vault. It at once–bold, expansive like the waters of the Missouri; vulnerable, tender as a precious dream–her aria resounded with fetching melancholy throughout the Nave from Narthex to Chancel. The song embraced every passageway and side chapel with a timeless, thought-provoking melody. Listening was rewarding both to mind and heart.

Then, at precisely **12.02 PM,** as on every day without overcast or storm since Blanche of Castile, the sun contributed a uniquely grand reflection to the colorful medieval stained glass windows recording episodes from both the Old and New Testament. This sudden burst of heaven's rays appeared to demonstrate God's approval of the gifted nun's work. She, bathed completely in ethereal light, Sister Genevieve finished her aria, curtseyed graciously to both audience and source of light, then withdrew.

"Awesome!" whispered Rolande, crossing her pretty legs opposite, readjusting the angle of her large chapeau. "No, *really* awesome! No, *really, really* awesome!"

Mass, at last, concluded with an organ piece composed by J-S Bach.

As the congregation began slowly filing out, some visitors stopped to snap photos of the *New Arena Chapel*. Beside its entrance, was located the miniature artist's tomb. The poignant yet straightforward epitaph chosen by her stepmother from **Matthew** read:

Marie-Pascale Kedari Castellane
XXXX– to –XXXX
"Be not Afraid."

More than a few in the departing crowd, especially women, knelt before the tomb already decorated with bouquets of fresh, bright blue tulips, white lilies, and red roses. They reverently pecked the inscription, piously touched the memorial.

"She was a saint!" whispered one pilgrim.

"Yes, indeed, she was clearly a saint!" agreed a second.

"We must all seek to be worthy of her sacrifice!" said a third.

"She was the Divine Child!" exclaimed still another young female pilgrim, gently yet firm.

Observing this semi-religious gathering from a distance, undercover police agents trying so hard to go unnoticed they were plain for all to see, frowned in disapproval.

Rising now to her feet, Rolande looked anxiously about the vast, crowded, vaulted Gothic Nave. How on Earth was she to find the *Good Ladies*? Especially, as she was at present just a speck in the human multitude? How, as well, were they to spot Rolande?

Lively, inquisitive, adolescent green eyes darted left, right, center and behind.

Up, down and around

Repeated their journey a second time

third

Fourth

Finally, the objective, or at least part of it, was located.

If Madame Castellane and Duchess de Charpentier were already departed, Sister Genevieve remained atop the central, high altar. She was accepting compliments modestly on her recent singing performance offered her by several *Old-Rich*, landowning couples. These titled aristocrats exuded with each studied-breath and practiced-physical motion an exclusivist, patronizing air. Like Prince Markovsky, these dapper-gents and stylish dames considered occasional public displays of religious observance a tedious but necessary requirement for maintaining their privileged social position and cultural solid, economic influence. A tedious undertaking perhaps, but still one these rarefied *Your Betters* need only perform on Christmas Eve and Easter Sunday.

Judging from both the forced-smile, otherwise-preoccupied way in which Sister Genevieve responded to this choreographed praise and the aristocrats' own unabashed insistence, this encounter be captured on neighboring television cameras, it was clear the nun was neither deceived by the fulsome compliments nor eager they be over-extended.

"Here! Look! It's me!" shouted Rolande, waving her arms to attract attention.

Breaking off her formalized chit-chat with the aristocrats, Sister Genevieve waved back. "*Yes, yes, Rolande, Sweetheart*"–her brown eyes signaled in recognition.

"Don't worry Rolande, dear!"–the vocalist in lime green explained further with her welcoming eyes. *"I already discussed the matter with Sister Claire and fully agreed you can do much to help us. You're precisely the person our cause needs at this crucial moment!"*

"Come! Come!"–nun motioned in kind, protective, elder sibling manner.

Unfortunately, the heavy crowds were not cooperative.

"Pardon"

"Pardon"

Slide

Slither

Excuse me," further begged Rolande, struggling through the multitude.

After only a few minutes, realizing the barrier could not be penetrated, she, with arms and face, delivered a gesture of apology.

Sister Genevieve motioned back sympathy. *"It would be so much fun if we could talk today, but I guess it's not meant to be."*

"Come back tomorrow, Sweetheart!" she, at last, made her voice heard above the rumble of departing feet. "Come back here tomorrow about noon."

"I promise I'll be there!" replied Rolande. "I promise I'll be here, then!"

A Pleasant Surprise

THE FOLLOWING MORNING, MARIE-FÉLICITÉE-ROLANDE-DE MONTFORT, wearing a short, light-gray skirt, soft-pink blouse, religious medallion around her neck, neutral-shade pantyhose, a white chapeau, and heels, exited the *Metro* station at the south opening to the Pont Neuf. The location placed our heroine parallel the Ile de Cité. Not far away on this Left Bank of the murky Seine, a large *Second Empire Period* water fountain marked the Boulevard St. Michel opening, or in local patois the–*Boul-Miche*.

As only to be expected on a Monday, the area was filled with camera-snapping tourists, committed-specifiers holding-forth atop boxes, eager pamphleteers, and industrious street vendors doing a most successful round of business. Classes recently adjourned at the neighboring University of Paris, crowds of students swarmed about as well. Boys were checking out girls, girls checking out boys.

The enchanting smell of fresh pastry and other distinctly French baked goods was clearly detected. At seeming never-closed, never-empty open-air restaurants, middle-aged male customers fervently debated the great issues of the day over wine or coffee.

Separating this famous plaza from the *Metro* station was a busy, congested thoroughfare possessing no stop signs.

"Eek! Blessed Virgin preserve me!"

Taking her life in hand, Rolande just managed to scamper across without being hit by any of the cars darting back and forth with no apparent regard for pedestrians.

If she at first navigating through self-absorbed contemporary times, Rolande soon discovered that after following one narrow serpentine street, then another, she was returned to the slower-paced, more reflective Middle Ages.

Along these less-trod, winding, cobblestone streets, only rows of closely packed, centuries-old, limestone, brown, and gray shuttered-houses with black undulating tiled roofs shared this young traveler's path.

While Monday was hectic for Paris in general, the tangerine, cocoa-brown and vermillion *Romanesque-Gothic* church of St. G is located in the 5th Arrondissement. This area preserved its usual pensive, comforting, calming personality. Approach to the basilica, so recently overwhelmed with vehicles and pedestrians, was now deserted.

No evidence remained of yesterday's multitude save for a few service programs dropped on the sidewalk. Entrance through the front portico revealed an equally peaceful, shaded interior. If a few electrical cords hinted at television's earlier presence, they were the only sign the agitated current age had ever once intruded.

Click, click, click–of Rolande's high heels in vaulted, granite Nave echoed long.

Not far distant could be seen the long rows of marble tablets inscribed with names of the church parishioners who died in *The Great War.*

Deep in thought, Rolande circumnavigated the Nave Once

Again

For yet a third pensive time, the *Click, click, click,* cli*ck*–of pensive teenager's high heels on granite resonated far.

"Oh! Mrs. Villers!" exclaimed Rolande in English upon finally observing another visitor within the great edifice.

Seated on a blue wooden bench just at left, she too dressed all in light pink, was Mama's new girlfriend, Iranian-American scholar Ashraf Kermanshani. Since moving to France after she'd been cheated out of the *Nobel Prize* for Mathematics and jealous rivals at her former university succeeded in blackballing her from any academic career in the United States, this expatriate sought anonymity both from the tabloid press and gossipy troublemakers through being known only as of the widow of famous Australian Medievalist Robertson Villers. Even if the *Montfort Ladies* were revealed the truth about

Ashraf's true identity and did much to promote her cause, one of their younger members, through force of habit, continued addressing the mathematician by her husband's name.

"Good morning, Mademoiselle Rolande," answered the erudite lady.

She motioned for *Missy* to sit down beside her.

Echo

Echo

"That's a lovely outfit you're wearing, Mrs. Villers!"

"Thank you, Mademoiselle Rolande. You're wearing a lovely outfit, *too*."

"I certainly did not expect meeting you here, Mrs. Villers." pursued *Missy*, eager to continue this unexpected crossing of paths.

"I come here often," replied the lady. She was also pleased at receiving this first opportunity to speak alone with the youngster. "I'm often to be found here."

"Really, Mrs. Villers?"

"Yes indeed, Sweetheart–at least twice a week."

Echo

Echo

Ashraf once more gestured for the girl to sit down beside.

Missy now complied.

She sat up straight on the bench, crossed her pretty legs, clutched *Coach* purse.

The hem of the girl's short dress receding.

"I'm not a Christian–let alone a Roman Catholic." illuminated Ashraf. "My older sister Golbihar and I, each born in Iran, were raised as Shia Muslims. However, materialistic American secular culture, Golbihar's daily practice for her Olympic figure skating career, and my study of mathematics combined to make our religion soon far more an ethnic identity than a faith. She is still living back in Amherst, Massachusetts. Golbihar continues attending Mosque in order to please our parents. As for me, I'm not sure that I still even believe in God, anymore! I certainly don't believe in *God* in the Koranic, Biblical, Hejira, St. Francis, Italian Primitives, Sistine Chapel, St. Therese of Lisieux sense. When I ask people'Where was God at Auschwitz? Where was God at Babi Yar?'–I only get uncomfortable, evasive answers."

"Yes, I've frequently wondered about that too, Mrs. Villers," concurred her young friend, she crossing her own pretty legs opposite, hem of own short dress again receding. "I often pray to God–asking Him why He permits bad things to happen to good people? Why He often permits the noblest of souls to suffer and the worst of scoundrels to go free? Unfortunately, God is yet to provide me with a satisfactory answer."

"Well, let's leave metaphysics to the philosophers, Mademoiselle Rolande. I'm a scientist. I only deal in observed, measurable, provable facts. Religion has never been my strong point or strong area of interest–"

Ashraf halted, anxious.

She crossed her pretty legs, opposite, Hem of her short dress receding.

The mathematician hoped she had not just given terrible offense. After all, Celine's offspring might very well share their mother's same deep, unquestioning religious faith. Her children might very well possess a similar conservative politics and orthodox worldview.

"Still, Mademoiselle Rolande," proceeded Ashraf, circumspect, "I fully realize we are now in a holy, sacred place. One, where God–no matter what form, guise, shape, or personality, He/She takes– can be found. From my first arrival in Paris, I've always found coming most refreshing, thought-provoking, and relaxing within these particular walls. I've discovered that sitting here surrounded by almost a thousand years of eventful history is an excellent way to get my plans in order for my next article in the journal, for my next speech at the academy."

"Yes, we are indeed inside a thought-provoking place, Mrs. Villers," answered the teenager in a reassuring, disarming voice. She was conscious of Ashraf's concern and was eager to put her friend at ease. "All this history and culture around us is sure to stimulate both mind and soul, Mrs. Villers."

"Yes it is, Mademoiselle Rolande."

"Maybe, Mrs. Villers," delicately ventured *Missy*, "maybe you actually do believe in God–follow the *God of Abraham*–much more than you even know? Perhaps, you've always been a believer but just never realized?"

"Perhaps you are correct, Mademoiselle Rolande. I know Madame Celine–your *Mama*–fervently wishes I become a believer."

This girl's encouraging thoughtfulness, her warm empathy, both qualities not usually found in strong-minded teenagers, led Ashraf to reveal far more than she originally intended.

The mathematician pointed to a devotional candle flickering beneath a centuries-old statue of The Virgin. "Your Mama even seeks the support of higher authorities in her quest to convert me." Next, opening her *Coach* handbag, she revealed the many pieces of literature about Roman Catholicism she received weekly in the post from Celine. "Your Mama wants me to read them all. She insists they will change my life."

Without a doubt, she devout mother's daughter, Rolande, listened approvingly.

"I am sure you will find them all most stimulating to read, Mrs. Villers! Mama would not have sent them unless she thought you would be interested,"

"Celine–*your Mama*–also wants me each day to wear *this*," explained Ashraf, now showing the religious medallion she was given by Celine at the chums' last visit. "I thought that to make Celine–your *Mama*–happy, I will wear it the next time we meet."

"Yes, Mama is certainly determined to convert you," observed Rolande with a musing smile. If voice politely noncommittal, this daughter strongly endorsed her mother's campaign to win a distinguished agnostic over to the Roman Catholic Church. "I never saw Mama so active in 'recovering lost souls' until she intends became friends with you, Mrs. Villers! Mama frequently tells me about how she must get you baptized before this winter. I think she wants to get you christened either Marie-Isabelle or Marie-Léonie. I bet in another time and place Mama would be a dauntless missionary in pagan climes–"

This time, it was Rolande's turn to stop short, fearing she'd just given offense.

Ashraf's disarming smile, her affectionate pat on the girl's right knee, indicated the youngster gave no slight.

Just down the way, at the entrance to the *New Arena Chapel* with its 64 near life size frescoes, was the grave of these masterpieces' pint-size creatrix. The *Messenger*'s final resting place was regularly provided with fresh, new, fragrant bunches of colorful blue tulips, white lilies, and red roses. Those contributing the bouquets and watching over the *Messenger's* grave discovered far more inner spiritual satisfaction could be obtained serving as the tomb's anonymous guardians than was ever possible through winning personal media attention.

Then, at precisely **12: 02 PM**, as on every single day without overcast or storm since the thirteenth century, storybook stain glass windows erected by Blanche of Castile seeming came to life as they were embraced with brilliant sunlight.

Rolande and Ashraf were each instantly engulfed in an ocean of stunning, magnificent, primary colors–the brightest of all red, orange, yellow, the grandest of any blue, magenta, green.

Running swiftly along the Nave's entire granite floor, a remarkable stream of multiple-shaded ethereal light soon also covered the tomb of Pascale Kedari.

This identical sunburst on glass panels occurred each day without overcast or storm since Blanche of Castile. In that case, eight hundred years of succeeding viewers could not help but be moved. Especially those spectators who were made active participants in this regular sympathy of joyous, otherworldly light. Today, Rolande de Montfort and Ashraf Kermanshani were two such active performers in the composition. As if they become the piece's s 1st violinist and its main piano player.

"Whenever, Mrs. Villers, I experience this marvelous show–am made part of it," confided Rolande, squinting, she covered head-to-foot in glittering, purest red, orange, yellow, the vivid pictures depicted in the windows dancing merrily on her adolescent body, "all my doubts about God's existence, or the rightness of His decisions, speedily vanish. It's as if God is reaching out to comfort me. 'Don't be distressed, Rolande, I am here for you, I am listening to you, looking after you.'"

The illuminated girl adding: "Surely, Mrs. Villers, something this splendid, this beautiful, can only be the creation of a higher, better, immortal force!"

"I understand why you and your Mama feel that way, Mademoiselle Rolande," replied Ashraf, she too squinting, she also covered head-to-foot in glittering, purest blue, magenta, green. Vivid pictures depicted in Thirteenth Century windows dancing merrily on her own graceful adult body. "This transcendent light does make you think, make you ponder, reconsider! It can make you feel as if we are each tiny but essential parts of some greater, higher, nobler, eternal force. One, that was here infinitely long before little you or I were born and sure to remain just as superb, heroic, infinitely long after mortal we depart! Call it *God* if we want–Call it: 'we embraced, contacted, touched by the *Abraham God*'–if we want."

Time passed.

Supernatural sunlight, at last, retreated. The ladies once more dwelt shadow.

"We really must discuss this matter together further and at length on another day very soon, Mrs. Villers!" urged Rolande with a wide smile, crossing her own pretty legs opposite. Suddenly, she felt herself in the company of a fellow spiritual traveler. "It seems that we both possess a mystical side, Mrs. Villers. One, which usually cannot locate an outlet–a place to express itself. Most likely, that mystical side of ourselves is usually unable to find a friendly ear, cannot find a comradely-tongue prepared to hear our brooding inner thoughts and eagerly discuss these and their own similar reflections."

"So true, so true, Rolande," replied Ashraf; in a show of intimacy, she dropping the formal honorific *Mademoiselle*. "However, Rolande dear, such friendly-ears–such comradely-tongues–do indeed, exist! Sometimes, as I've discovered in the case of you and your excellent

Mama, these precious soul-mates come upon us when and where we least imagine or expect them!"

Ashraf pressed the girl's right-hand lovingly firm.

"I enjoy coming to this church as a scientist, too," she continued, crossing her own pretty legs opposite, hem of own short dress again receding. "I enjoy studying the perfect geometrical design comprising the Nave, the Vault, the Transept, the windows, and every other shape forming this near thousand-year-old structure. If the Twelfth and Thirteenth Century builders lacked knowledge of modern engineering, they certainly understood geometry and its power. Theoretically, this structure should have collapsed eight centuries ago. Yet because the Medieval builders obeyed perfectly the laws of timeless geometry, their edifice still stands–stands grandly."

Ashraf paused.

She pecked Rolande on her lips.

Pecked Rolande's lips again.

Ashraf continued holding the girl's right hand, tight, protective.

"Whenever I am frightened or unsure of myself, Cherie, I come into this church to regain my confidence. After resting here within these walls awhile, I know, I can then easily overcome any obstacle or problem our hectic, self-absorbed contemporary world puts before me."

"Perhaps, that's because God wants you to fulfill a mission, Mrs. Villers?"

"Maybe so, Cherie."

"Maybe so, Mrs. Villers"

Minutes passed.

"Look! Look, Cherie!" signaled Ashraf, motioning across the way, she, at last, releasing her young soulmates hand. "The person you likely came here this morning to see has just arrived! Why don't you now go and have a merry visit with her while I continue my brooding."

Firebird

MARIE-SABINE-VÉRONIQUE CASTELLANE WAS VISIBLE in the Chancel at the basilica's far end. Like Celine de Montfort and Ashraf Kermanshani, Firebird too was in her early-thirties. This morning, she wore an unbuttoned light pink cardigan over a short, sleeveless, pattern dress, neutral-shade pantyhose, white heels. A wide chapeau was atop her head with fetching face and shoulder-length cherry-blond locks. The serene, multicolored glow emanating from the Thirteenth Century stained glass windows provided a slightly ethereal aspect to this lady's presence.

"I guess Sister Genevieve already decided to accept me," surmised Rolande, observing that the nun she came to see this morning was absent. "I presume Pascale Kedari's stepmother is going to be less sure I am up to the mark! She must have insisted, she is the one to meet me this morning, instead."

"Well, here goes," Rolande whispered anxious setting off to be evaluated. "I hope I can pass the exam!"

Firebird was deep in thought, her left forefinger studiously following the winding natural black line in the Chancel's off-white marble floor. Her right hand rested contemplatively at her strong chin. Crouched on knees, hem of short dress retreated several additional inches, and her magnificent legs were now even more visible. From age sixteen until her mysterious, unexplained retirement at just twenty-six, those same pretty lower limbs enabled Firebird to become the greatest ballerina of the century.

"So, this is the child Rose, and the two Sisters are so enthusiastic about!" silently commented the famous dancer, she furtively raising her brown eyes to observe the approaching teenage newcomer. "So, this is the one even agnostic Professor Eisenberg is so eager I come to know!"

Aware she was being appraised, Rolande made a deep curtsey, a humble smile.

"This new child is roughly the same age my own *Little Marie* would be today," thought the urban martyr's stepmother. "This new child possesses the same bubbly, energetic, idealistic personality as my own *Little Marie*. This new one may not be a painter like my Sweetheart, but she too is an auto-diktat, a child born with special gifts she learned to hone herself. Instead of Art, this new girl concentrates on history and literature."

"Yet," the judge quickly appended, "this child is also the daughter of that conniving, scheming, whore Madame de Montfort! In addition, if my Sweetheart was a virgin, she, like the two nuns dedicating her mind and body entirely to God, this other creature is obviously–*more worldly, experienced*!"

Rolande again made a deep curtsey, projected a humble smile.

Well, it's sinful of me to be so harsh without even really knowing the child!" Firebird scolded herself, clutching the religious medallion bearing an image of Saint Therese of Lisieux on her necklace. "I must investigate further before making my final judgment."

Light from the stained glass windows gave Firebird's hose an attractive shine.

"Good morning, Madame Castellane," ventured the teenager, anxious. "I am so glad we can finally meet."

"Do you know anything about geology, Mademoiselle Rolande?" queried Firebird. She still crouched on her knees. Her brown eyes are continuing to carefully follow her left forefinger's journey along the natural black line in the Chancel's off-white marble floor."

"No, I am afraid I don't, Madame Castellane. My fields are primarily history, literature, and political science."

"You are a famously learned child. Geology should not be left out of your wide expertise."

"I promise to look into the subject, Madame Castellane. It sounds ever-so fascinating."

"Good, good. Just like my *Little Marie*, you are not only smart, gifted, and energetic but also respectful of your elders." She soon adding: "That's a nice outfit you are wearing today, Mademoiselle Rolande."

"And that's a nice outfit you are wearing too, Madame Castellane." "Thank you. You're a gracious young lady." Firebird paused contemplatively.

The light emanating from the stained glass windows gave her hose an attractive shine.

"I never went to school."

"I never went to school, either, Madame Castellane," intimated Rolande.

"Where I come from, girls are kept at home."

"Where I come from too, girls are kept at home."

"No formal education for us is permitted."

"No, Madame Castellane. No formal education for us is permitted."

"How did the adults always explain it to me when I asked why I could not accompany my brother Richard to school?" recounted Firebird. *"Girls are not supposed to be educated. All girls will ever need to know can much better be taught them at home. Education ruins a girl's natural tenderness, natural obedience, her simple, deep unquestioning faith. The school will only fill a girl's impressionable little brain with **concepts, theories,** and **notions**. Education will make a girl want to wear trousers. It will make her talk-back, cut her hair short, smoke pot, become a socialist, a hippie, not attend Mass."*

"Those are almost the exact same words with which Mama scolds me, Madame Castellane!" interjected Rolande eagerly. Soon adding: "But simple, *uneducated* girls like us still manage picking up a few facts on our own, do we not, Madame Castellane?"

"Ah, yes! So we simple, *uneducated*-girls do, Dear!" observed Firebird, offering the newcomer a comradely smile. "So we both do! Even if we are never permitted to go to school!"

Echo

Echo

"When no one was watching," continued the prima ballerina, she still crouched on her knees, still investigating the natural black line in the marble, "we simple, *uneducated*-girls both read–*still do read*–all kinds of scholarly tomes and learned periodicals. One subject I personally found–*still do find*–especially fascinating is geology. I've over time developed a strong amateur interest in this subject. Geology is not simply the categorizing of soulless rocks. Instead, the story of God's world. For instance, the stone we are standing upon this morning dates from the *Precambrian Epoch*. During that hectic period aeons ago, our planet went through tremendous earthquakes, frequent meteor-bombardments, and experienced great volcanic activity. France and Europe did not even exist yet! Dating from the formation of the earth approximately 4.58 billion years ago and lasting until roughly 600 million years ago, the *Precambrian Epoch* stone is the oldest around. It's in this time that we first find granite, basalt, quartz, and dolomite."

"Don't you think it's only fitting" suggested Firebird, still crouched on her knees in short skirt, her brown eyes and left forefinger yet studiously following the natural black line in the altar's marble floor, "that these most ancient of stones should be used to build our church? Employing this kind of material celebrates–makes manifest–the power, mystery, and glory of God our lord and savior."

"Amen! Indeed, it does, Mme. Castellane!" concurred, Rolande.

"Who are those crazy Protestants in America who claim people are damned to Hell if they don't believe the earth is only 6,000-odd years old?"

"Born-Agains, I believe, Madame Castellane."

"Ah! I don't know what troubles those silly people. God could have created the earth any time He wished! 4.58 billion years ago just as well as six thousand!"

"Quite true, Madame Castellane. God could have created the world any time He wished. Creation over aeons speaks more of God's power, mystery, and glory than any folk-tale invented by mortal man."

"Now, you are starting to sound just like my martyred-Sweetheart!" laughed Firebird with an approving smile. "You are starting to sound just like my own *Little Marie*."

Without a doubt, Rolande was performing well on her test.

Across the way, it four meters square, the area roped-off, the workers currently off to lunch, was an opening in the Nave floor. It represented an excavation dig. One, directed by Madame Castellane's polymath brother.

"Under different circumstances," explained his sister, proudly, "my Richard would be a celebrated archeologist like Sir Howard Carter or Heinrich Schliemann. On multiple occasions, I've tried persuading Richard to accept an appointment as a tenured professor of archeology. It would be a position allowing him to lecture students in class and provide him all the funding needed to continue leading successful expeditions in the Middle East. Perhaps, he can then discover a lost civilization, finds a new King Tut's Tomb or the City of Troy! Such distinguished positions have already been offered to him. They've been offered not merely by the University of Paris but also by the University of Louvain in Belgium and by the University of Heidelberg in Germany. However, my Richard insists he cannot abandon his flock at St. G."

"My brother's goodness, my brother's spirituality," sighed his protective sibling, "often gets in the way of him fully expressing his many intellectual gifts." She is soon reflecting: "Even though my Richard is the *educated* one of our pair, even though my Richard is clearly the smarter one of our duo, his naive, home-bound sister is nevertheless so often required to look after him–to employ her own meager abilities, limited experiences, to keep Richard's distinguished head screwed on straight!"

Véronique mused.

"How could men ever manage in this world without women present to look after them!"

"Yes, Madame Castellane" Rolande concurred. "How could men ever manage in this world without women present to look after them!"

"Still, this seems to be the way God intends it. Women are supposed to be the helpers, not the deciders. Men are to take the lead– After all, God sent us His *son*. Instead of winning outward glory, it appears women are to obtain fulfillment through assisting others–" She paused. "But Madame digresses."

Echo

Echo

"Father Richard is indeed a most learned, gifted person, Madame Castellane!" insisted Rolande. "I've long made sure to read all his brilliant articles in the scholarly quarterlies I subscribe to. I save them, too, in my library?"

She is venturing: "perhaps one day, Madame Castellane, you would like to come over for a visit and see all my books and periodicals? When you do, you'll see how I've gotten all of Father Richard's article's bound into hardback?"

"Maybe, I should come and visit."

"I'll be most honored to receive and guide you through, Madame Castellane. Mama calls it the **Missy Collection**.*"*

The prima ballerina smiled, contemplative.

Mutually pensive moments elapsed.

"Currently," resumed Firebird, her voice grown maternal, she gesturing for the pair to observe the roped-off excavation site across the way. "Currently, my Richard is investigating what lies beneath our church's floor. Political events at present are making him unable to resume his digging in the Middle East. He's doing it here in Paris. I hope he finds something interesting."

Rolande saw it appear her decisive chance.

She seized it firm, grand.

"Madame Castellane?"

"Yes"

"Did you know St. G is actually the third church built on this site?"

"Really, sweetheart!"

"Indeed, Madame Castellane. The original sanctuary was built in approximately AD 150 by the first Christians to live in France–then called Gaul. The Romans destroyed it during the persecution launched by Diocletian in the AD 290s. A second and larger church was erected on this site by Clovis and the Merovingians in roughly AD 500. This present–the largest and most beautiful one–was erected by the

Capetians in about AD 1050. Of course, Blanche of Castile– one of my favorite people in history–expanded this third church even further in the early 1220s."

"The majority of people at the time were illiterate and could not read the Bible of course," continued Rolande with all teenage exuberance. "So, Blanche of Castile ordered the windows to depict major episodes in the Old and New Testament."

"*See,*" instructed Rolande, directing Firebird to look at various colorful, elaborate glass panes. "*See.* Here, for instance, you've got: *Adam and Eve–Jacob wrestling with the Angel,* or with God, who, by the way, cheats through delivering Jacob a blow, not in the rules–*Moses coming down from Mount Sinai with the tablets–Joshua making the sun stand still–Deborah–Ruth and Naomi–David slaying Goliath–The judgment of Solomon–Job–Daniel in the lions' den–the Annunciation–the Nativity–Christ driving the moneylenders from the Temple–the Crucifixion.*"

"In this way," summarized Rolande, "the great Queen Regent hoped that worshipers could understand what the Bible recorded even though they could not actually read it."

"Fascinating!" observed the prima ballerina, she deeply impressed. "You are an ever-so learned and masterfully interpretative child!"

Then, for the only time in history, heaven issued a second glow through the windows of Blanche of Castile.

Rolande was instantly engulfed in the purest of red, yellow, and orange, embraced by the finest of blue, magenta, and green.

The splendid images in thirteenth century stained glass became vividly alive.

The characters in the Biblical stories merrily danced upon and across Rolande's body–*Adam and Eve; Jacob wrestling with God; Moses is coming down from Mount Sinai with the tablets; Joshua; Deborah; Ruth and Naomi; David slaying Goliath; Job; Daniel; The Virgin confronted by Gabriel; the birth of Christ; His expulsion of the moneylenders from the Temple; the Crucifixion.*

Rolande not simply recorded these stories on her body. She was soon herself brought within the dazzling Medieval panorama.

If any supernatural endorsement of the girl was required, she now received it.

Firebird interpreted this to be.

Standing up, at last, adjusting her dress, chapeau and cardigan, the prima ballerina smiled welcoming, tender.

Opening her arms to offer the young supplicant a warm, protective embrace, the great dancer cried: "Come to me, Sweetheart! Let Madame Castellane give you a kiss! Let Madame give you a big, long hug!"

Time passed.

A distant old clock with ancient sounding bells now struck **12:30**.

"Before you become our cause's new heroic leader, Dear," counseled Firebird, pressing Rolande close, "you first need to have some lunch."

Allegro

TIME PASSED

Seasons change

Events transpire

Ferdinande de Godefroy, now Duchesse d'Aveyron, gave birth to a son.

After completing her latest foreign tour, Countess Marie-Therese Celine de Montfort delivered a recital at the Garnier Opéra in Paris. She played: Concerto no. 12 in A by Mozart, Sonata in F-Minor "Appasionata" by Beethoven, Concerto in A opus 120 by Schubert, Concerto in F-Flat by Liszt, and Concerto No. 3 in F-Minor by Rachmaninoff. When this magical lady commanded the keyboard on all previous occasions, central Paris was jammed for hours beforehand. Traffic came to a standstill, and the *Metro* was hopelessly clogged. Fans (of both sexes) fought like cats and dogs to obtain a ticket, any ticket, for the event. It was a scalpers' nirvana. For those unable to enter the ornate *Second Empire style* hall and hearing the performance live, *CD*s were available at all major stores and on *Amazon* within a week. People unable to locate the fast sold-out regular copies eventually found pirated versions produced in China, South Korea, Vietnam, and Thailand.

"So did I do well, Brigadier Aslan?" asked the *Good Little Soldier.* She, wearing a long, strapless, sapphire color opera gown while being driven back to cream shade No. 3 Rue Artemis following her latest memorable concert performance.

"You were splendid, Mme. Celine!" replied the famous warrior, proudly at wheel. "Splendid!'

"Really, truly, Brigadier Aslan? You really, truly thought I played well?"

"Yes, of course, Madamme. Celine! I've never seen or heard my favorite birthday girl deliver such a grand performance as this evening! Your precious, dainty fingers were made for the ages! You are the finest pianist of them all!–As well as the prettiest and the best behaved!"

"Bless you! Bless you! Bless you, Brigadier Aslan!" squealed the *Good Little Soldier*, her long cherry blond hair now fallen in her face. Reaching forward from the beige passenger row, she gave her champion a devoted hug, next, showered him with heartfelt kisses. "Remember, I owe all my success entirely to you and your constant help and encouragement!"

"Bah! Nonsense!" insisted the spymaster with deep paternal affection. "I could tell my Mme. Celine was born for the piano the moment we first met. If I have done anything at all, it was merely to hone a peerless, God-given talent that already existed slightly."

"I still love, admire, and above all *depend on you*, Brigadier Aslan" giggled Celine, she clutching her hero just as tight. "No matter what you say, Brigadier Aslan, you are the crucial reason for all my success!"

"Well, Child, if you continue insisting on loving and admiring me so much, then please let me loose for the moment and sit back like a proper birthday girl. We are approaching some heavy traffic, and my hands need to be free and firmly at the wheel. I certainly don't want my gifted little darling who so depends on me to end up in a car accident!"

"I always promise to respect my elders, Brigadier Aslan" answered Celine. Her smooth, unblemished bare arms and shoulders obedient if regretfully releasing the amorous clutch, she retreated to the vehicle's passenger row. "I will have plenty of time to hug and kiss my hero when we get home."

"That's my good Child!"

The long, black, shiny feline stretch limousine advanced down the avenue.

Honk, honk

Beep, beep

"Ooh! Mercy-me! Goodness, gracious! The Virgin be praised!" Also sitting atop the beige leather passenger seat was the latest edition of *La Croix*. One headline instantly caught the pianist's eye. "Ooh! Did you see this, Brigadier Aslan? Did you see this, Brigadier Aslan?"

"Pardon? What are you speaking of, Mme. Celine?" was a knowing answer.

"Here's a color photo of our little wandering book collector! A major article, too! While I was away on my latest piano tour, it appears that our *Missy*, with the assistance of her new radical feminist chums at St. G Church, was really up to something! Our *Missy* is making quite a name for herself and her noble cause! The newspaper records all of *Treasure*'s so dedicated, so Christian activities! Ooh! Mercy-me! Goodness, gracious! The Virgin be praised! It all makes a parent feel so-so honored!"

"Didn't I tell you that our *Missy* possesses a glorious *Calling*?" replied Brigadier Aslan. "Didn't I tell you that any daughter born of such a remarkable Mama's womb is bestowed a glorious *Calling*!"

End Of Part One

Like The Fall Of Singapore

IRANIAN-AMERICAN EXPATRIATE SCHOLAR ASHRAF Kermanshani, or to her neighborhood: *Mme. Prix Nobel*, clad in light pink, exited her apartment building. It was a russet color five floor structure located in the quiet, residential 7th Arrondissement near the green, verdant Luxembourg Gardens. The urban sky slowly changing from topaz to sapphire-was clear. Not a single white cloud was seen above. In the far distance, a brilliant tangerine orb queenly retreated behind centuries-old gray and brown limestone battlements. Following the long, scorching summer at last mercifully passed, belated autumn in the French capital was pleasantly dry, softly cool. A mild, refreshing breeze traveled the early evening city air.

Wearing a short, thin dress, Ashraf enjoyed sensing the gentle breeze stroke lovingly her body. When this physical touch was combined with delicious aromas emanating from nearby restaurants, the experience was particularly gratifying. A peek at her *Cartier* watch announced *6 PM*. Dinner at cream color No. 3 Artemis with Countess de Montfort was arranged for *7:30*. Her chum set out this early so that instead of later taking the crowded *Metro* or an expensive cab to destination, she might stroll there, and the process takes in the benefits of nature. As she promised earlier in the church, Ashraf tonight wore the religious medallion she received from Rolande's mother.

"Don't move!"

"Don't say a word, bitch, or you're dead!"

Two huge young men in battle fatigues slammed Ashraf against a wall.

Gripped by neck, arms, stomach, she'd break in pieces if pressed any tighter.

A cold, soulless, piercing, metallic dread invaded her entire body.

This horrible sensation raced head to foot; then, foot to head; next, back again.

Ashraf felt lost, abandoned, forgotten.

A sickening, loathsome terror seized her heart, lungs, and intestines.

One, made still worse by the fact this nauseating fright could not be described.

When she, at last, trying to scream, a soldier covered her mouth more firm.

If in the past imaging the bravery she'd display at such a time, when this event actually occurred, she instead froze with crippling terror.

"No, no, it's not what you think, Madame!" counseled one soldier, apologetic, he quickly perceiving the reason for Ashraf's concern.

"No, no, Cherie! Unfortunately, Jean's right," said the other young trooper speaking in a lustful, threatening voice. "There's no time for that now! Maybe later, though, when we get you in a more amenable mood."

"Shut up, Paul! Madame's scared enough as it is!" reprimanded the first soldier, much annoyed. "Now, let's go quick!"

In one swift motion, the soldiers threw a heavy blanket over Ashraf's head, cast their bundle into a waiting military supply truck, jumped into the vehicle, and sped off.

Unspecified time passed.

Paralyzed with foreboding beneath heavy, filthy bedding at the back of a military van, trying to collect her jumbled thoughts, Ashraf was unable to calculate the exact period elapsing. Was it thirty minutes, forty-five, an hour? More? Less? She couldn't now or in the future, say.

Slowly, slowly, as no further assault occurred, the kidnap victim regained a modicum of clear reasoning. "If they were going to rape me," she speculated, "they would have already done it. Or, murder me, too!" She soon, adding: "At least *I hope so.*"

The lorry, victim, and abductors aboard trundled on.

"Where am I going? Where am I being taken! What's going to become of me?" pondered Ashraf. If she is still frightened, her heart and lungs nonetheless slowly, slowly throbbed less quick; her arms and legs gradually, gradually relaxed their clinch. Suppose she was lying silently, motionless on the floor of the military truck under a large, thick, dirty covering, her eyes tight shut, all as yet impenetrable darkness;. In that case, she could at least hear freely. Employing that one sense still at her command, Ashraf hoped to discover both her own approaching fate and the progress of events outside.

After long travel at seeming fast, steady pace down an unobstructed thoroughfare, the van suddenly pulled-up short. The driver next led the big vehicle in one direction; soon, propelling it along a different path. Finally, the military transport advanced at a steady but much slower pace, straight ahead. Outside, the arrival of other big vehicles was increasingly detected, the cry of orders shouted, the growing thud of feet in combat boots. Above all was heard, the frequent, unnerving eruption of gunfire.

At last, the van halted near the whirr of helicopter wings. Apparently, tonight's deed was well-practiced, all its participants save the victim, were ready to move at a moment's notice. Like clockwork, the two soldiers now jumped from the truck's driver compartment, raced to the back of the vehicle, opened it, swiftly removed the bundle containing Ashraf, and only seconds later placed it aboard the waiting army helicopter.

"Got her in, Paul?" queried the more gentlemanly soldier as Ashraf, still covered in a thick, dirty blanket, was dropped unceremoniously on the floor of the chopper.

"Yes, Jean! We've got Cherie ready for her next trip."

"Now go!" shouted Jean to the chopper pilot. "Go! Go! Go!"

The chopper was off.

Rising above the landing pad outside Paris, it headed east.

How long did Ashraf lie prone on the floor of the chopper? Forty-five minutes? An hour? Maybe longer? Perhaps, shorter? Only God is certain. Yet exhausted both in mind and body, Ashraf neared her mysterious fate, resigned. "So, I guess *this* is *it*. If your number is up, I guess your number *is up*."

Additional images from the past, ones not normally expected to arise in traumatic situations, also came to Ashraf's mind–

Her daughter Rebecca who died so young

Her older sister Golbihar queenly atop the Olympic gold medal ice

Tristan and Iseult

Celine and *The Ladies Garden Trust* Then, a last sweet memory returned –

"I love you, Mr. Villers," Ashraf murmured, even today still addressing her lover with honorific and informal V*ous*. "I love you so much, Mr. Villers. I will always be your faithful little girl, Mr. Villers. I hope I've made you proud of me, Mr. Villers."

She reached out as if to clutch her hero's arm again, to rest her needy cheek on his welcoming, protective shoulder.

She fell unconscious

I

When Ashraf finally awoke, the chopper was descending just outside Coblenz in the German Rhineland. This was the base of the French 3rd Mechanized Armor Corps under the command of General Pierre Marchand. A crack NATO army unit, a veteran of at least a dozen successful foreign campaigns, it could, if the word given, reach Paris within hours. The battle-hardened, armed-to-the-teeth French 1st Paratroopers, also under General Marchand's command, could secure possession of all the capital's administrative, transportation and utility sites even sooner.

After the whirlybird landed, waiting soldiers hustled haggard Ashraf into a jeep and drove her to the unit's command headquarters situated in an adjacent Medieval castle.

In every direction, to the right and left, up and down, both near and far, belligerent humanity was on the move. As sergeants and junior officers shouted instructions, massive tanks and armored personnel carriers lumbered into position; long lines of eager, highly disciplined infantry marched forward; huge pieces of artillery and loaded missile launchers were eased onto flatbed trucks and train rolling stock; fighter jets swooped low overhead. An electric sense of both excitement and foreboding engulfed the cool, refreshing autumn evening air. Oddly, the atmosphere was no less cheerful, exhilarating, as it was worrisome, threatening.

"What's all this about, Monsieur General?" questioned Ashraf several minutes later, she disheveled, out-of-breath yet still trying to project confidence. Following her arrival at the brooding castle, the Iranian-American was summarily pulled from the jeep, next, dragged through an iron-gate, then, hustled down a long, dark, damp hallway before at last, she brought before several grimacing, uniformed, fortyish men seated behind a wooden table covered with yellow lined writing pads and fat manila envelopes. "What's this all about, Monsieur General? Some of your underlings abruptly grabbed me off the street in Paris. As a woman, I first naturally guessed the thugs had something much different in mind. Thankfully, I now gather not. Anyway, what's this all about, Monsieur General?"

"Just in case this bloke isn't really a *general"* thought Ashraf, "perhaps supplying him this promotion might set the scoundrel in a more charitable frame of mind toward his prisoner!

"Aren't you named *Ashraf Kermanshani*? Weren't you born in Tabriz, Iran?"

"Well, yes, that is the name with which I was born. Since becoming a legal resident in France, though, people address me as *Mrs. Robertson Villers,*" replied Ashraf. Glare on her interrogator's face instantly demonstrated that, *general* or not, he was not swayed by idle flattery. "Yes, my sister Golbihar and I were also both born in Tabriz, Iran. However, my parents took us to 'The States' when I was just six. I have only gone back to Iran on one occasion. That visit wasn't in recent years, of course!"

"Why do you live in France under an assumed name?"

"It's not *an assumed name*–it's my late husband's name. You might have even heard and read of him. A brilliant scholar Mr. Villers was, God bless him! He was as loving and protective of me as he was learned, wise! A good number of Mr. Villers' splendid books and magazine articles are also translated into French. One was actually made into an independent movie! Mr. Villers wrote the screenplay! I directed it, too! The film won him both the *Golden Palm* at Cannes and an *Oscar* at the U.S Academy Awards! It's now easily available on *DVD*! People compared Mr. Villers' films with those of Fred Zinneman and Billy Wilder! The president of France later made Mr. Villers a member of the Legion of Honor! Mr. Villers bought me a new gown to wear when I accompanied him to the ceremony! It all makes a girl like me–Mr. Villers called me his 'faithful little mate' –so rightly proud!"

"According to our information, you are still *Mademoiselle Kermanshani*."

In France, every respectable woman upon reaching age twenty-five is given the honorific *Madame* whether she is married or not. Calling thirty-three-year-old Ashraf *Mademoiselle* was therefore unpardonably rude, insulting. It was the equivalent of calling her *Bitchy Old Maid* or *Cheap Tart*.

"Well," Ashraf continued, ignoring the obvious slight, "it is true that Mr. Villers and I never got around to officially tying-the-knot. Still, we definitely lived as husband and wife. We certainly viewed and treated one another as husband and wife. It wasn't a mere tax or real estate scheme. I can tell you the name of many persons both public and private–here and in The States–who will testify to this."

"Be that as it may, you are living in France under an assumed name!"

"I suppose so. But it's just a technicality."

"Law cannot be dismissed as a *technicality*. Without law, there is no civilization. Without law, there is anarchy, chaos! As a foreigner living and working in France under an assumed name and counterfeit marital status, you are guilty of breaking an entire series of laws. You reside and operate within our borders under false, possibly malicious pretenses! How cannot you expect the authorities to come after you eventually? Come after you, rightly!"

"I never meant any harm," pleaded Ashraf.

Not satisfied with such an answer. The interrogator scribbled down some lines on a yellow, lined notepad.

What did he write? It looked ominous. Mr. Villers would know. He could read upside-down. Unfortunately, his wife never acquired that handy skill.

A second officer behind the table next spoke.

"According to our information–information supplied to us by the most reputable public and private sources both here in France and in, as you say–'The States'–you fled to Europe after being discovered belonging to a highly dangerous and very active Iranian-financed Islamic terrorist network. A deadly, Tehran-directed, Jihadist group pursued by police and intelligence organizations on four continents."

"And who exactly are all these grand, illustrious *sources* who accuse me?'

"We are not required to tell you, Mademoiselle."

"And just what evidence do they bring against me?"

"We are not required to tell you, Mademoiselle."

"May I speak to an attorney?"

"Only to an attorney we select."

"May I speak to someone from the United States embassy?"

"The United States embassy has already been informed of our decision to arrest you. It says it does not choose to intervene in a fellow NATO member's domestic affairs."

"So I can neither obtain independent representation nor confront my accusers? Aren't the right to independent representation and the ability to confront one's accusers pillars of the very law you are so determined to uphold?' The very law to which I am supposedly such a threat!'"

"These are emergency circumstances. In emergency circumstances. Other rules apply!"

About to scream in frustration, Ashraf thought better.

This was no time to come off as just another pushy-American.

She tried a different tactic.

"Look, commanders! Would I be wearing these kinds of clothes if I were an Islamic terrorist?" entreated Ashraf, *Playing Dumb*. She gestured to her now crumpled short, low-neck designer dress, to her tore sheer hose, scuffed heels. "I've never once touched, let alone fired a pistol! I've never even seen a bomb! As all my friends, neighbors, and coworkers can testify, the mere sight of a roach throws me into a tizzy! As for a mouse? Well, I promptly jump on a stool and scream bloody-murder until I'm rescued! It happened to me once at night, and my frantic caterwauling woke up the entire building! I almost needed to be taken to the nut-house."

"A crazy, witless *flibbertigibbet* like me," jabbered Ashraf, "is the last one on Earth people would select to carry out a terrorist plot! Or, to participate in anything complicated, for that matter!"

The judges were unmoved.

"We expected a figure as notorious and dangerous as you to be traveling in disguise. Your flirtatious antics might fool the Anglos but not us!"

A long, typed, official-looking form was presented.

Sign this!"

"Sign *what*?" queried Ashraf, exhausted from her damsel-in-distress performance.

"Your confession."

"*Confession* to me having done *what*?"

"Committed espionage," answered the judges.

"*Espionage?*"

"First, you confess that while serving as an agent for a foreign power, you repeatedly penetrated the highest levels of the French government. Second, you confess to stealing **Top Secret** diplomatic and military information. Third, you attempted to obtain France's nuclear codes. Finally, you acknowledge often attempting to influence French domestic policy in order to assist your Iranian-funded international terrorist network!"

"But that's ridiculous!" exclaimed Ashraf.

"This will go a lot easier for you if you cooperate, Mademoiselle."

"And suppose I refuse to sign?"

"This will go a lot easier for you if you cooperate, Mademoiselle."

"Yes, but it would be a lie."

"Sign now, and you might at some later date be exchanged."

"Exchanged to *where*?"

"Iran"

A commotion erupted in the corridor.

"We've got both of them, now, Sir," informed a junior officer.

"Good, good" remarked the first judge, rising to his feet. "Formal signing of the confession can wait until later. That's, after all, just a formality. Much more critical is that henceforth we've got all the plotters in our hands."

Ashraf looked around.

Two pairs of troubled feminine eyes linked.

"Celine, darling!"

"Ashraf, precious!"

Exhausted, shoeless, disheveled, Countess de Montfort staggered into the room.

The women embraced

Pair clutched tight.

Each held her companion desperately fast.

Two souls brief become one.

"I didn't betray you, Ashraf!" pleaded Countess de Montfort when at last she able to speak. "Please, please, believe me! I would never betray you! This must've already been arranged. The scoundrels must've been after us both!"

Heart and lungs still racing, she repeated: "Please, please, believe me, I would never betray you!"

"No fear, Celine," promised Ashraf. "I never thought you betrayed me."

"I love you."

"And I love you, *too*."

"*See,*" indicated Ashraf in an effort to further bolster her friend's spirits. "*See.* I've got on the religious medallion you asked me to wear daily."

Bless you! Bless you, Ashraf!" replied Celine in appreciation. "I guess I have at last succeeded in making you a Roman Catholic! It's at times like these that we need our faith most!"

The pair again embraced.

Clutched tight.

Each held beloved companion desperately fast.

Both sought the comfort of another sovereign being.

"Take them away," instructed the first military judge, referring to the prisoners. "Let them keep company with the rats for a while. After that, I am sure they will be more cooperative."

II

The cell door slammed behind the two women.

Celine's right stockinged-foot touched a big, long, furry object.

The object returned a loud, angry squeal before slithering into soupy darkness.

"A rat!" exclaimed Celine, recoiling in terror. "A rat!"

As she cringed, additional large predatory rodents snarled before they too beat a hasty retreat to confer on how the vermin next assault these human intruders.

"Rats! Rats!" winced Celine. "In this dreadful hellhole, they are at least two feet long! Nothing is more filthy, is more loathsome, is more disgusting in all of God's creation! I'm sure that even the Blessed Virgin hates rats!"

"We might need reconsidering," discreetly counseled Ashraf. "Lord! What do you mean?"

"Have you gotten a tetanus shot in the last five years, Celine?"

"Yes, last month *Missy,* Ferdinande, and I went to Father Richard's clinic together."

"Good! My own physician says it's best to keep up-to-date on tetanus inoculations."

"I agree. Why do you ask?"

"Mr. Villers was present at The Fall of Singapore–Remember *The Bridge on the River Kwai*?"

"Oh, sure!" answered Celine. "Starring Sir Alec Guinness, William Holden, Jack Hawkins, Sessus Hayakawa! Directed by David Lean! Produced by Sam Spiegel! Seven Oscars! That's a terrific picture! *Missy* has it in her DVD collection. I love *The Bridge on the River Kwai*! It's one of my absolute favorites! And I'm a crybaby girl, too! *The Bridge on the River Kwai* is certainly not a crybaby girl movie. No! No! No 'triple-hankie films' for me! I can also still whistle the famous theme! That's back when they made tasteful, inspiring, thought-provoking movies! Not this current sex, gore, fantasy drivel!"

"Well," said Ashraf, growing circumspect, "Mr. Villers–he was then *Major Villers 1st Australian Fusiliers, VC DSO OBE*–was present at The Fall of Singapore in February 1942. He told me that the Japanese would permit him and the other 140,000 prisoners to only eat bugs and rats."

"I read about how in Singapore the Japanese machine-gunned all the hospital patients, pregnant women and old people, how the Japanese tortured right-and-left, how they gang-raped little girls, used infants for target practice. Why are the Japanese constantly so mean? It must come from all that 'Children of the Sun,' Samurai, Bushido nonsense."

"'Anyway,'" replied Ashraf, "Mr. Villers told me that after having nothing else to survive on for three-and-a-half years, 'one discovers those furry buggers actually don't taste half as horrible as you originally expect.' Mr. Villers insisted, 'fried rat possesses a memorably *pungent* flavor.' One, uniquely its own. ''Those little critters, Mate' Mr. Villers told me, 'are the unsung heroes of the Empire! In their own *pungent* way, they are no less responsible for our ultimate triumph than victory in the Battle of Britain or at Alamein!"

"Lord! Are you driving at what I think you are?"

"Yes, Celine. We may not be at The Fall of Singapore, but we too are clearly in trouble. I don't know if you and I will be in this cell for three-and-a-half years, but it doesn't look like we'll be leaving any time soon. I also suspect feeding us is no longer a priority for our own captors than for the Japanese holding Mr. Villers. Therefore, like it or not, Sweetheart, I believe it's best we start establishing closer relations with our *pungent* neighbors."

Several large, predatory rodents slithered past.

These creatures, stopping briefly to size the women up.

"Maybe, they also want *closer relation*s with me!" thought Celine.

III

"Another human presence was detected in the damp, soupy, rat-infested darkness.

"Hello? Hello?" cried Ashraf, leery.

"Who's there?" questioned Celine, apprehensive. "Who's there?"

With eyes still unadjusted to the murky, dank, gloom, the women perceived this new arrival as a mere disembodied whisper or source of faint scratching.

"Hello? Hello?" repeated Ashraf with mounting suspicion. Remembering her earlier experience on the street with the troopers, she grasped her friend close so that she and Celine might defend together against further lustful male advances. "Hello! Hello! Tell us who you are! Tell us who you are right now, or I'll, or *we'll scream*–"

She fell silent, realizing the futility of the situation.

There was no sense threatening to scream–who would care! The rats?

The Japanese?

"No, no, don't worry, it's only me–Professor Eisenberg!" reassured a mysterious, distinctly female voice. One, growing louder, view of the gray form issuing these words becoming sharper upon approach. "It's me, Professor Eisenberg!"

"It's you!" exclaimed Ashraf with tremendous relief, still holding Celine to her bust. "Thank God! I–*we*–thought you were someone else."

"No, no, it's only me, Mrs. Villers," reassured Matilda.

"I am so glad we can finally be introduced Professor Eisenberg," interjected Celine, adopting a lighter voice. "*Missy* often speaks of you."

"Favorably, I hope, Countess de Montfort?" replied Matilda, demure.

"Oh, yes indeed! My daughter speaks very well of you!" answered her mother. "Nevertheless, I long imaged Professor Eisenberg would be some kind of wild-eyed, fire-breathing, Leftie-Feminist who cuts her hair short hair and wears trousers. Thankfully, it appears you are not!

"Don't believe everything you're told, Countess. I subscribe to *Vogue* and go to the beauty salon, too!"

The pair giggled.

Matilda-Gisela Eisenberg–leader of the reformist bloc in the National Chamber of Deputies and Marie-Therese-Celine de Montfort– mistress of the conservative status quo! Until now, two such radically opposed individuals seemed unlikely ever crossing paths either in this world or the next.

"And *I,* Countess," replied Matilda, "long imagined *you* were going to look like Marie Antoinette, Eva Peron, or Imelda Marcos!"

"Don't believe everything you're told, Professor." The pair giggled.

"I used to have the same kind of thoughts," revealed Ashraf, unconsciously applying grateful strokes to the medallion of the Virgin around her neck. "I once referred to Celine as *Messalina*."

"Don't believe everything you're told!" the trio laughed in unison Three fiends each fell on their knees. Pecked one another on lips.

Hugged tight.

Each stroked her companions' long, thick, hair.

Three swayed gently, softly, as one being.

Hummed a beloved Bob Dylan tune.

In fact, these latter-day musketeers were yet to catch sight of one another. So impenetrable was the soupy darkness, the cavaliers recognized mutual presence only through touch and sound of a voice.

III

Vermin slithered.

Roaches made merry

"How did you also end up in this godforsaken rat hole, Professor Eisenberg?" questioned Countess de Montfort, also in her early-thirties.

"Please call me *Matilda,*"

"Provided, you call me *Celine,*"

Girls giggled

They embraced tight.

Pecked lips.

"I was seized at my office at the University, Celine. I was grading essays when these paratrooper thugs suddenly burst in and dragged me off. When I finally arrived at this castle, some kangaroo court declared I was guilty of 'committing espionage.' They claimed I was tampering with government documents, trying to steal nuclear codes, aiding a terrorist cell–or some similar rubbish!"

"I was arrested by some uniformed goons too, Matilda," replied her new aristocratic chum. If in blackness unseen, the women's bodies were only inches distant. "Thank God *Missy* and Ferdinande were not there! The girls probably would have been swept up in this roundup also."

The countess soon adding: "The charges against you, Matilda, sound just like those leveled at me."

"It appears as if we're all in the same mess under the same trumped-up charges," observed Ashraf, she understands that as frightful as her own recent experience was, it represented just a single element of a far larger operation."

Vermin slithered.

Roaches sped the walls.

"Did the soldiers make you sign anything, Matilda?' "They wanted me to sign a confession but I refused." "I refused as well," replied Celine in the soupy night.

"I also wouldn't sign," said the Iranian-American mathematician.

"That's about the same time I was hustled out to meet you in the corridor, Ashraf" reminded Celine. "As I recall, the officers were actually more interested in humiliating us than in obtaining our confessions."

"Remember what that scoundrel ordered?" reminded Ashraf. She then, from memory, reciting what the judge told the other officers: "*Take them away. Let them keep company with the rats for a while. After that, I am sure they will be more cooperative.*"

"They are expecting to break us," said Matilda. "They think they can force *Witless Women* and *Fragile Females* to sign or say anything men wish."

IV

"Well, don't fear, my little girls!" now interjected Countess de Montfort, she gripping the medallion of the Virgin around her neck. The pianist's earlier weak, frightened voice abruptly grew maternal, fiercely protective. The Grand Courtesan now summoned forth the power of all her mighty ancestors–those celebrated in portraits from Michelangelo, Raphael and Vermeer to Corot, Degas, and Picasso. "Don't fear my children! We are believers! We trust in God! Those soldiers are about to be in for a big surprise!"

Celine pressed her companions to own body as a mother gathers in her children during times of danger. "This is all my–Mama's– responsibility. Mama needs to take command. In the end, the army is really after me. You poor sweethearts were sucked into a crisis, not of your own making. The army thinks that if I am captured–that if I am removed from the scene–if I am no longer available to give him uncredited advice, that miserable weakling President Markovsky will panic. Unable to make up his own mind, Markovsky will do anything he's told. The army thinks it can then force me to make a video tape instructing the wretch to allow the army into Paris."

"It's a coup!" exclaimed Matilda.

"And after the army is securely in control," surmised Ashraf correctly, "it will then turn its attention to finally suppressing the Pascale Kedari opposition once and for all."

"Well, just you watch, my little girls!" assured Celine pressing her companions closer to own breast amidst the soupy, impenetrable darkness. "Just watch, my children! We are not going to break! We are not going to crack no matter what the blackguards do to us! Courage is not the monopoly of men! As the Japanese soon discovered at The Fall of Singapore, girls can be heroic, too! Girls can be brave, too!"

"Yes, Mama, we'll show them!" cried Ashraf.

"Yes, Mama," seconded Matilda. "We'll show them that girls can be just as– maybe even more brave, heroic–than men!

"And Mama promises her darlings," said Celine, "that we three won't be the only girls to stand up and be counted as brave, as heroic!"

Betrayal

SINCE 1958, WHEN GENERAL de Gaulle chose to live in a private residence with his family, no president of France has ever slept at the Elysée Palace. The country's elected leader frequently devises international policy, often formulates domestic legislation, holds summits, and entertains foreign dignitaries at this Baroque mansion in central Paris. Yet when daily work is done, the French chief executive now goes home. As a fabulously rich financial tycoon, Prince Markovsky had no trouble following this newly hallowed tradition. Although, his sprawling, walled-off, baronial estate on the outskirts of the 16th Arrondissement, was certainly not what *The General* had in mind for the family home of a democratically elected president.

Surrounded by huge manicured lawns and well-tended *Continental* style gardens, the rambling Seventeenth Century palace at this mini-kingdom's center might easily strike viewers as being once the residence of an absolute monarch. Such a supposition is quite understandable considering the manse earlier belonged to Louis XIV's influential mistress and morganatic wife Madame de Maintenon and later to Louis XV's renowned flame Madame de Pompadour. After the *Revolution*, Napoleon, Talleyrand, Madame de Stael, George Sand, Chopin, and still later Sarah Bernhardt, Clemenceau, Debussy, Edith Wharton and Colette all spent holidays or directed government affairs here. Fallen into disrepair after 1945, the palace and its extensive grounds were purchased a decade ago by Markovsky with part of the proceeds from one of his many insider-trading Wall Street, junk-bond, leverage buy-out deals.

Originally taken on just for money-laundering purposes, Celine de Montfort's Thursday evening gentleman caller soon developed a deep affection for his new domain. Today–with its pipe and electrical systems updated; it introduced central heating; it supplied all the most cutting-edge gizmos and gadgets; the palace's superb art collection now open to guided tours; the grounds frequently rented for scenes on television or in movies; the chateau often the site of UN or diplomatic conferences–this estate is once more both a tourist's **Must See** and a citadel of conspicuous consumption-political power.

So much did Markovsky enjoy residing on this exclusive piece of real estate, he often did not travel into central Paris or visit other major French cities for weeks. During earlier periods, such physical isolation might place the president at a serious political disadvantage. However, in the age of the Internet, cable television, and social media, Markovsky had no difficulty maintaining the support of his core following and exerting influence over the larger public from a distance. *The General* might not have holed himself up in such a reclusive manner. But then again, *The General* did not have Twitter or Facebook.

I

A telephone erupted with an unhappy, anxious wail in the darkness.

Jolted from a pleasant dream, Markovsky fumbled for the receiver.

At last, his right hand located the goal.

"Hello? Hello?"

"Monsieur President?"

"Yes"

"I am sorry to call at this hour, but there is a report you must hear at once."

The glowing face of a nearby clock announced **3: 25 AM.**

"Christ! Can't this somehow wait until morning?" pleaded Markovsky, irritated.

"I am afraid not, Monsieur President."

"Very well, goddammit! Go ahead then, and this better be worth it!"

"Just a moment, someone else wishes to speak–"

Across the line were detected conspiratorial whispers, nervous shuffles of feet.

"Monsieur President" now spoke a more authoritative yet equally worried voice. "This is General Mercier, the Defense Minister."

"What do you want, General Mercier?" queried Markovsky. "And more important what do you want of *me*? Especially at this appalling, godforsaken hour!"

"Army Group 3 at Coblenz is threatening to move on Paris."

"Is this a bad joke?" snarled Markovsky, lamp near bed turned on.

"No, Monsieur President. I only wish it was merely a joke."

"Well, you are the Defense Minister, General Mercier. Things like supply, morale, and discipline are your department. You could have easily dealt with this insubordinate grumbling alone. Besides, what has the army to complain about! I've already given them three hefty salary hikes, praised them to the skies, and pledged I wouldn't be pushed around by those filthy Americans! I also provide the generals every last new weapon or battle game they wish to play with!"

"Army Group 3 at Coblenz is threatening to move on Paris."

"You mean this is a *coup*?"

"That appears correct, Monsieur President."

"A coup!" cried Markovsky, sitting up straight in bed. "Goddammit! This is the kind of thing you expect from niggers in Chad! Well, we're not niggers in Chad! We're whites in Europe! Coups aren't supposed to happen anymore in civilized countries! Besides, I thought the French got this sort of thing out of their system with Algiers!"

"It seems not, Monsieur President."

"So can't you quickly send in other troops to stop these rebels?"

"All the other army leaders instructed their men to stand aside–not to intervene."

"What about the air force? Won't they strike the traitors?" "The air force," explained Mercier," also will not intervene."

"Surely, the navy is loyal?" implored Markovsky. "I thought the various armed services hate each other? Don't they look for every opportunity to show each other up?"

"The navy, too, is standing back, Monsieur President."

"So, this means the military is abandoning me? Do they want me out of office?"

"Not precisely, Monsieur President.

"Then what-in-all-hell do the instigators of the coup want, Mercier?"

"They wish you to concede to certain demands, Monsieur President. If you accept them, the military says it will stand down."

"If I *concede to certain demands*, the military says it will stand down?"

A new voice spoke from across the line.

"Monsieur President, this is Kellerman, your Minister of the Interior and Domestic Intelligence. I have taken the liberty to order the sealing-off of all harbors, airports, central train stations, major bridges, large tunnels, and significant border routes. I' have also dispatched police units to secure the national television and radio headquarters. However, since this whole process cannot be done in an hour, both I and General Mercier each believe you must–we repeat you *must–* deliver a televised message to the people of France. One, assuring them that their elected government remains in power and desires the peoples' immediate assistance at this critical moment in our history."

"Can we announce," urged General Mercier," that Monsieur President will soon address the entire nation?"

"I'll get back to you," said Markovsky.

After hanging up, he turned to the other side of the mattress to grab a second telephone. This one has linked directly to No. 3 Rue Artemis.

Ring, ring, ring, ring, ring, ring, ring

"What-the-Devil is wrong!" growled Markovsky with mounting anxiety. "My Celine picks up no later than the second ring! Where's my Celine! Where's my Celine!"

Ring, ring, ring, ring, ring, ring, ring

"Hello," at last responded a peremptory male voice.

"What son-of-a-bitch are you?" snapped Markovsky. As far as he was aware, this particular line of communication was known only to himself and one special feminine chum. Politicians, diplomats, journalists, celebrities, cartoonists, and standup comics all speculated this private link existed but no one in the public, or so the president thought possessed proof.

Visible through the bedroom's right bay window after sunrise-was the site of the garden party where teenage Rolande heard a still, small voice.

"Let me speak to Countess de Montfort at once!" ejaculated Markovsky.

"Countess de Montfort has been placed under protective custody," came the reply.

"What's that supposed to mean! Let me speak to Madame, at once!"

"Countess de Montfort has been placed under protective custody."

"And when will she not be, as you say: *under protective custody?*"

"I am not permitted to provide such information." "Do you know who you are now addressing?"

"Yes, the President of the Republic."

"Well, fuck you, too!"

Markovsky hung up.

"Christ! The coup plotters discovered about Celine and me!"

If attacked, the regime could quickly seal off all the nation's harbors, airports, central railroad stations, major bridges, and large tunnels. In response to a serious military challenge, the administration could fast secure the country's media headquarters and close down all border routes. Finally, when threatened with invasion, the president might use television to rally the population to his side and against the interlopers. Yet even when all these actions were taken, how could the Markovsky government ever possibly hope to survive when it denied the aid of the *Montfort Ladies*?

"What do I do? What do I do?"

Pacing meditatively inside a bedroom with *Chippendale* furniture and Elisabeth Vigée Le Brun portraits of bewigged grand lords and corseted noble dames looking on from cloth-of-gold papered walls,

Markovsky was deeply agitated. Too upset, realizing he was no more clothed than at the moment his mother bore him.

What do I do? What do I do?"

If he is walking at the heavy tread, a large, colorful, ornately designed Persian rug absorbed the sound.

"What do I do? What do I do?"

Or, more accurately: *"What would Celine tell me to do?"*

At that instant, like Adam in the garden, Markovsky knew that he was naked.

II

"What should I do? What d should I do?"

Then rudely arrived for him the apparent revelation.

Set above a waxed, mahogany *Chippendale* chest-of drawers with lace coverlet stood a framed color photograph of the French president during his recent trip to India. On that occasion, Celine accompanied him under the guise of a translator. In this picture, the lovers were seen riding an elephant. Seated atop the great pachyderm, each wearing a *British Raj* outfit, the pair might be mistaken for a Nabob and his Memsahib in a Rudyard Kipling or E.M. Forster story. Normally, Markovsky quite enjoyed gazing at this 8-by-10 glossy. It reminded the often harried-chief executive that there still exist nicer climes and more pleasant environs. At this particular moment, however, he suddenly found the image highly irritating. It has an intense pain to observe.

While the photo depicted Markovsky gripping tight the rearing animal's reins, he struggles mightily to keep the willful beast in place for the cameramen, Countess de Montfort, in contrast, cross-legged like Scheherazade, appeared as stunning, regal, and beneficent as a Mogul empress. While one of her delicate, gloved hands secured a huge Edwardian chapeau in position, the other, queenly offered her anxious, beleaguered, clearly inferior caste gent, refined if unchallengeable instructions.

"No wonder the military wants me out!" snarled Markovsky, he looking away embittered. "The generals probably imagine that I belly dances to her and intend committing suttee if Celine dies first!"

"But no more! No more!" he cried, shaking his fist at the bewigged grand lords and corseted noble dames seeming to watch him from portraits along the bedroom's papered walls.

"How could I have allowed this to happen!" further wailed international-Lochinvar, European-Romeo, Prince Alex. He, usually renowned for his skill at managing women. "I never suspected it for a moment! She had me! Took me! She played me as if I was her concert piano!"

The seducer had been *seduced*,

the ravisher, *ravished*.

The negotiator, *negotiated*

If his many achievements since coming into Celine's genteel orbit were, in fact, all of the lady's doing, Markovsky had until now been oblivious. Not even once did the *New General de Gaulle,* as he liked viewing himself, ever suspect he owed his entire public career to Celine. Rather than an immortal statesman, this Napoleon-wannabe was, in truth, as newspaper cartoonists often depicted him, just the grand courtesan's yo-yo.

"Damn her!" shouted the president, still naked.

Instead of confessing his grudging respect for Celine's immense backstage skill, admitting reluctant gratitude for all the success she provided him unacknowledged, hedonist Markovsky expressed only embarrassed male rage. Vanishing too from his narcissist mind was a remembrance of all the precious happiness, warm companionship, and critical emotional support Celine bestowed him along the way. The terrific sex, as well!

"Damn her! Damn her!"

If only a handful would ever know for certain about the President's indebtedness, the truth was nonetheless out. And like a jinni released from a bottle, out forever!

Closing his eyes, Markovsky visualized the dirty dozen generals and cabinet ministers privy to the truth. They, henceforth, snickering at him, sharing malicious jokes whenever the President was not looking.

See! I always thought it was Madame de Montfort who wears the pants!

See! Look at the way the lady controls him like a marionette!

She can make him dance about like an organ-grinder's monkey!

For all his purported macho qualities, Markovsky is really only that woman's toy!

And the strutting peacock is too full of himself to ever know it!

Heedless of the consequences of breaking with the individual who both created and preserved his career, Markovsky turned on Celine. Better, he thought, obtain short term gratification for a fragile masculine ego than maintain the loyalty of one's best and surest ally.

Upon at last wrapping in a patterned, silk kimono to cover his shame, the chief executive rushed to the bed and grabbed the first telephone.

"Mercier! Kellerman! Set all the cameras up! Call in the scribblers! Announce a press conference. Report that the President of the Republic is about to address the nation and the world on an issue critical to all!"

Next, to his defense chief, Markovsky instructed: "General Mercier, inform Army Group 3 Coblenz and their supporters that the President of the Republic is eager to consider the military's well-founded and most patriotic requests."

Lord, make me too, an instrument

NEITHER FERDINANDE DE GODEFROY nor Rolande de Montfort was caught in the military roundup. While succeeding in placing Ashraf Kermanshani, Matilda Eisenberg, and Celine de Montfort under arrest, the coup plotters failed to get their hands on the Countess's two daughters. As a nursing mother and as the wife of the Secretary-General of the *United Nations*, Ferdinande could not be nabbed without provoking an international uproar. However, her far more politically vulnerable younger sister escaped the generals' clutches only through a keen eye and lucky accident.

Uneasiness was almost palatable in greater Paris during the seventy-two hours proceeding the attempted coup. This unsettling atmosphere was found both on the street and in the home; it was detected in suburban neighborhoods no less than cosmopolitan venues. The malaise possessed an imperceptible yet definite heaviness. Mounting fear, growing dread of the forthcoming event might almost be touched, tasted, even smelled. Every finger, tongue, or nose within one hundred miles of the French capital understood a calamity was at hand. If visually, life functioned unchanged, every eye knew a terrible menace approached. Never before or since did the metropolis and her millions of inhabitants so ready themselves for peril. When the putsch actually occurred, it came almost as a relief.

Celine's *Treasure* knew this foreboding well. As Countess de Montfort's daughter, she was born to dwell perpetually at the vortex of all major political and social events. There was no way this teenager could avoid the impending conflict. Added to this was the effect of her loyalty to the Pascale Kedari reform movement. Finally, Sister Claire and the other *Five Good Ladies* recently selected *Missy* as *Little Giotto*'s new public champion. All these factors gave the young redheaded book-collector much cause to feel a probable target of political reaction. As hours, then days passed, she became ever more nervous when telephones rang unexpected, doors or hinges creaked, lamps abruptly went on, or, the girl received glances from passersby on the boulevard.

In the end, such worry actually served *Missy* in good stead. Approaching cream color No. 3 Rue Artemis on the evening of the third day, the girl suddenly observed gray military trucks parked outside the townhouse's front entrance. She spied troops sealing off the area to curious pedestrians.

"Good lord!" whispered *Missy,* halting just out of sight. "They've come for me at last?" And where was her mother? They've likely taken Mama, too!"

Before the troopers could notice, this redhead in a short blue dress raced down the street in the opposite direction.

Forward,

Forward

Quick

Still, quicker–*Missy* hurled herself down the chosen path. She first crossed one block; then, a second; next, a third; now, a fourth. In the daytime, this region was a familiar neighborhood. It characterized by long rows of elegant, white, ionic-columned, neoclassical townhouses. These impressive structures ran parallel on opposite sides of peaceful, upscale, residential streets. Running parallel too, if each separated by fifteen paces, were tall, wide-branched chestnut and plane trees. More than a few noted figures in European history once called this stately community home. However, in the waning light of urban sunset, a fresh, clearly defined, well formed neighborhood was transformed into thick, soupy, almost impenetrable blackness.

Rather than gingerly following a route known since earliest childhood, *Missy* was compelled to fumble along a dark, uncharted path. One, navigable only by carefully tracing the course of what was now become unfriendly, just vague-proportioned gates and walls. More than once, the dainty voyager stumbled at unseen street corners.

"Where should I go next?" the teenager speculated, the gloom so thick, her hands moving along a limestone wall only two feet distant, were invisible. "I must find a place that's prepared to take me!"

When she, at last, maneuvered through this somber environment, *Missy* exchanged it for the far better lit though seeming perpetually traffic-congested Rue de Rivoli in arcaded, fashion-setting boutique, tourist **must-see**, central Paris. Upon discovering a momentary lag in the surging torrent of vehicles between Palais Royale and the Louvre, the girl dashed across the busy avenue as fast as a short hem dress, a wide chapeau held in place by a single pin, and high heels could allow.

"Eke! Blessed Virgin preserve me!"

Scurry

Scurry

Scurry

After somehow managing to reach the far side without being run-over, or her frantic lunge across the busy thoroughfare caused lasting sartorial embarrassment, our young lady next calmly traversed the broad, well-lit, and above all car-free, Place Hotel de Ville. Her path carried her north to south. From the balcony of the off-white, brown, and gray Renaissance style city hall giving the plaza its name, General de Gaulle on August 25, 1944, proclaimed *The Liberation*. A huge television screen was being erected nearby so that crowds of deoted football fans might watch the French national team compete against Germany in the final, deciding match of the *World Cup*.

"Now I know where I'm going. I'm going to St. G Church. I know Sister Claire and the other *Good Ladies* will take me in!"

Crossing the murky Seine north to south over the Pont St. Antoine, *Missy* reached the Left Embankment. If the river was murky at night, its black surface glittered a galaxy of brilliant individual points of the reflected city light.

"Sister Claire and the others are likely expecting me! Yes, they're most likely expecting me!"

While cars raced the boulevard, pedestrians strolled the balustrade-sidewalk, and customers merrily chattered at outdoor restaurants, each-seeming oblivious to all but themselves, *Missy* understood with growing certainty a climatic event was at hand. One, which demanded to play an essential role in its summation.

"Oddly," Mademoiselle de Montfort reflected, "this evening's flight from the authorities only makes me more sure of what I've got to do next!"

If begun the race in panic, she approached its finish line with ever-gathering confidence and determination.

"'Be not overcome by evil,'" *Missy* recited from **Romans**, "'but overcome evil with good.'"

"The world is a closed door, a barrier," she quoted Simone Weil. "Yet it is also the way through."

After progressing along the riverbank for about twenty minutes in view of massive *Gothic* churches and leaping spires, then, passing within sight of the Conciergerie: the vast, turreted, seven-hundred-and-fifty-year-old fortress built by Phillip the Fair, she and the king's citadel each illuminated by regular streetlamps and aerial gun searchlights, *Missy,* at last entered the narrow, serpentine, cobblestone, Medieval pathways of the University of Paris. It is better known as *The Latin Quarter* or the 5th Arrondissement.

"Here, I am at last," she cried after reaching the front portal of *Romanesque* St. G. church. "It's not too late! I know God never sleeps or locks his door to anyone.*"*

I

When *Missy* first visited several months previous at noon, the large tangerine, cocoa brown, and vermillion basilica again looked empty save for its new arrival. This evening, with Vespers, completed a half-hour earlier, no further services were scheduled until the following morning. At night, rather than exhibiting living biblical stories and embracing viewers in oceans of magnificent primary colors, the eight hundred-year-old windows of Blanche of Castile were obscured in darkness. Shadow now covered much of The *New Arena Chapel*. After sitting pensively for a time atop a green wooden bench, *Missy,* still apparently alone, rose to her feet and began circumnavigating the church's huge, cross-beamed vault interior.

Up and down

North to South

East to West

Around again

Journeying a third time

Then, a fourth

click, click, click, click, click–of pensive high heels on granite resonating far.

"Blessed Virgin," implored *Missy*, "please look after Mama–Please look after Ferdinande and her husband the Duc d'Aveyron and their new baby boy Henri–Please look after Auntie Philippine and Auntie Léonie and Brigadier Aslan–Please look after Sister Claire and Sister Genevieve and Mme. Castellane and Father Richard and Duchess de Charpentier–Please look after Mrs. Villers and Professor Eisenberg–Please look after all our loyal servants–Please take care of all the widows and orphans and refugees and political prisoners and displaced and persecuted and misunderstood people here in France and across the world–Please look after Simone Weil, wherever her noble soul now journeys–"

"Please too, look after Mrs. Jackson and her two daughters and all the other people who asked me to be their guide when I was on my travels," continued *Missy*. "Please Virgin, look after the bookseller in Angers who sold me the biography of Pascale Kedari–And please look after any others I can't presently think of–Yes, please forgive me, God, for not remembering them at the moment. I'm so very sorry for my poor recollection."

Click, click, click, click, click–of pensive high heels on granite reverberating far.

Yet if even Simone Weil and St. Therese confessed to nagging doubts, how could a Montfort Lady dare assume she possessed more ability to accomplish the deed! Why should a courtesan be more confident of victory than a saint?

Missy fell to her knees, closed her eyes, clasped her two hands, and made a rare personal request. Tomorrow, she was required to carry the banner of *Little Giotto*'s reformist cause throughout this troubled world. She hoped she was up to it.

"I never follow men's icky politics, Lord," began *Missy*, "and I certainly don't intend starting now! Besides, as Mama frequently tells me: 'Politics is no place for a lady.' However, this movement which the good Sisters and their friends are encouraging me to join is different–It has nothing to do with the men's icky politics, Lord– rather, this movement is actually, in a manner, about–*You–*"

She paused, wracking her teenage brain for the proper phrase and metaphor.

"Blessed Virgin!" further prayed *Missy*, she only half sure she had settled on the appropriate words and sentences. "I've been entrusted by the good Sisters and their friends with a mission. The good Sisters and their friends are convinced that only I can perform this particular mission. Please, Queen of Heaven, give me the strength to carry it out successfully. Above all, My Gracious Lady, please give me the strength not to disappoint those who are depending on me."

"No need you fear lacking the strength to carry out your mission, Cherie!" assured Sister Claire, arriving from the left."No need you fear being a disappointment to us!"

Missy's fellow redhead wore: a wide lapel jacket with padded shoulders; a skirt with hem above knees; a frilly white blouse with ribbon at collar; neutral-shade pantyhose; black high heels. Save for a silver crucifix around her slender neck and a wedding ring symbolizing her eternal marriage to Christ, this lovely lady in her mid-twenties might easily be mistaken for a professor, an attorney, a physician, a business executive, or any other dynamic young secular career woman. If French, was the Brit's second language, no listener could tell.

"Besides," added the renegade-duchess, she still speaking in faultless Gallic tongue, "Sister Genevieve and I never personally selected you with a mission. We only made you aware of the task for which God had already chosen you! Since God never sends a believer on a *Fool's Errand*, we also never doubted Cherie would succeed. And succeed grandly!"

"Have you been here long, Sister Claire?" asked *Missy*, a little abashed at discovering some of her most intimate thoughts overheard. "Were you listening to me chattering away with God for a long time?"

"Only a little while," replied Sister Claire. "I confess I much enjoy watching you *chatter away* with God. I also confess to taking every opportunity. I'm sorry if I make you uncomfortable. It's simply that so few individuals possess your unique level of intimacy with God. So few are granted the privilege to able to *chatter away* with the Almighty!"

The Red Virgin adopted a tender, nostalgic, maternal voice.

"As a matter of fact, the only other person I ever met possessing such deep mutual intimacy with God is, *was,* my Little Giotto. No wonder it didn't take long perceiving you two precious children, you two special kids, are soul-mates. No surprise, I quickly understood God selected you to lead martyred Pascale's cause to victory!"

Missy debated how best to answer.

Earlier, while she was yet battling pangs of indecision, still confronted by the fear of failure, Sister Claire's optimism would have sounded most unsettling. However, these same cheery observations proved the final push *Missy* needed to conquer all remaining doubt.

"Very well," the teenager meditated. "Perhaps I'm not today, nor will I ever be equal to St. Therese or Simone Weil. Yet feeble, imperfect, sinful creature that I am, God has chosen me, anyway. I guess He'll be satisfied if I can only do my flawed utmost!"

"Bless you, Sister Claire!" exclaimed *Missy*.

She gave her friend a long, warm, fervent hug.

"Bless you, Sister Claire, for having confidence in me! I love you, Sister Claire! I love you, awesome!"

And I both love and have confidence in you *awesome* too, Cherie."

Echo

Echo

II

"I definitely know you will make us all proud, Cherie," interjected a spirit with a magical singing voice, she approaching from across the Nave. Like Sister Claire–the former British aristocrat, Sister Genevieve–the plumber's daughter from Rouen, wore: a light-gray jacket with padded-shoulders; a skirt of the same shade with hem above knees; a frilly white blouse with ribbon at collar; neutral-shade pantyhose; black high heels. Save for a silver crucifix around her slender neck and a wedding ring symbolizing her eternal marriage to Christ, this second attractive lady in her mid-twenties might easily be mistaken for a professor, an attorney, a physician, business executive or any other dynamic young secular career woman. In fact, just days before, she had returned from Quebec after fulfilling her assignment to open her religious Order's first branch in North America.

"Sister Genevieve!" exclaimed *Missy* with delight. "It's awesome to see you've come to be here, also! Must've been a long flight from Canada? Are you still tired out from the journey!"

"Oh, I'm perfectly fine now, Cherie. I'm no longer tired. As it turned out, thinking about seeing you again made the flight seem much shorter."

Echo

Echo

Missy curtseyed deep.

"Now come here at once, Dear!"

Teenager complied.

Opening her purse, Sister Genevieve removed a fresh hatpin.

"I must get Dear's so beautiful yet so unsteady chapeau secured."

"Thank you, Sister Genevieve. I'll be most grateful for your assistance. My chapeau was almost blown away when I needed to race across Rue Rivoli."

"There," proclaimed the nun after her work on the adolescent's headgear was complete.

Now it supported by two hatpins, *Missy*'s fashionably chapeau need no longer fear sudden gusts of wind.

"Mme. Castellane is in the kitchen now," informed Sister Genevieve, checking her watch. "Since Pascale died, her stepmother has lacked anyone official to fuss and worry over. She asked me earlier if she might cook us dinner this evening, and I agreed. So, before we take any further action to change history, let's first enjoy Mme. Castellane's famous cooking."

"Yes indeed! We certainly cannot miss one of Mme. Castellane's splendid dinners" observed Sister Claire in strenuous approval. Then, addressing *Missy*, she instructed: "As I used to frequently tell Pascale– 'You shouldn't take on the world with an empty stomach.'"

Before leaving, the three friends stopped respectfully at the opening to the *New Arena Chapel* with its 64 priceless life-size frescoes. Just beside the entrance to this sanctuary was *Little Giotto*'s final resting place. *Be not Afraid*–counseled the epitaph from **Matthew** atop a tomb covered each day with fresh bunches of anonymously contributed white tulips, lilies, and roses.

"Would you please be so kind as to leave me alone for a few moments, Sister Claire, Sister Genevieve?" asked the teenager. "I hope you don't mind, Sisters. I want to make a prayer–I want to make one, alone."

"Ah, but of course, *Sweetheart!*" replied Sister Claire with a protective smile. "Certainly, you can be alone now. You and the Almighty need to "have a chat."

After each is providing their charge a maternal kiss, the two nuns withdrew.

Missy knelt before Pascale Kedari's grave.

At that instant, one could sense the presence of the Holy Spirit. This transcendent force was as clear as it was also invisible, as distinct, tangible as it too, inaccessible, forever beyond grasp.

Missy prayed to her otherworldly companion.

"Blessed Virgin, please make me your instrument! Blessed Virgin, please make me, like Mademoiselle Kedari, an instrument of your everlasting glory!"

Dinner

"IT'S POSITIVELY AWESOME, MME. Castellane!" exclaimed *Missy.* "You have truly outdone yourself this time, Mme. Castellane! This is a feast for the ages!"

Seated with her too around the dinner table in the Baroque rectory building were: Sister Claire Preston; Sister Genevieve Fauré; Duchess de Charpentier; that lady's now twelve-year-old adoptive twins Marie-Delphine and Marie-Albertine; and Father Richard Castellane, Each, seconded *Missy*'s opinion with either own wide smile or own additional words of enthusiastic approval.

"Thank you very much, Cherie," answered Firebird, she visibly touched by the compliments. Her long, sinuous cherry blond hair was tied back, and her short magenta color dress was covered by a veteran, sauce-spattered, gray apron. "I am delighted you approve of my cooking. I am so happy to at last receive an opportunity to give you a hearty meal."

If training since her earliest years to adorn the international stage left this greatest of prima ballerinas a highly marginal, a quite selective, finicky eater, the famous dancer enjoyed few things better than creating banquets for others.

Along with three of the dining room's four papered walls could be seen framed lithographs by Marie-Pascale Kedari. Beginning with small, imitative, childlike interpretations, these works steadily advanced in power, self-confidence, and ingenuity. The pictures soon projected a bold, vivid, thought-provoking style all their memorable own. This increasingly sophisticated series of images recorded the swift development of an exceptional, untrained creative genius. One, tragically cut off from the world just as she approached the apex of her talent. Esteemed critic Cardinal Casimir Blanchard often urged that the lithographs should be placed in a museum, but the artist's stepmother insisted the prints remain just where her daughter intended.

"I made some of my *Little Marie*'s favorite dishes for this evening" reminisced Firebird, stirring a large stainless steel pot after first adding diced red onions to the fragrant, brewing stew. "My Sweetheart taught me how to do the recipes herself. Exile that she was, my child always found food a keen, pleasant reminder of home. At first, Darling needed to escort me personally to all these various ethnic food shops in far-flung immigrant neighborhoods. Then, she needed to watch over my efforts in the kitchen closely, give me constant instructions. It was, at first, quite complicated, time-consuming, intricate. The empathetic kindness she showed me, won Cherie a place in Heaven with all the saints and angels! But in the end, even a silly *Flibbertigibbet* like me got the system down pat. Now–just imagine!–tonight it all comes like clockwork."

The prima ballerina paused.

Then, smiled nostalgically.

She wiped away happy tears.

"It's too bad that my Sweetheart is not around any more to see how her *Scatterbrains* Mme. Castellane has so mastered the process. My child would now be so very proud of me!"

Kashke Bademnjan–ground eggplant; Kosher curdled milk; vinegar; salt; cayenne pepper; fried Persian rice; garlic; turmeric; olive oil; walnuts; caramelized onions; lemon.

Ghormeh sabzi–sliced chuck roast; rice; white onions; potato paste; spinach; fenugreek; salt; kosher butter; turmeric; saffron; olive oil; kidney beans; cilantro; parsley; dried lime

Gheymeh–lamb cut in cubes; split yellow peas; red onions; salt; cayenne pepper; tomato paste; zereshk; dried lime, turmeric; saffron; parsley, vegetable oil; rose water; orange

Fesenjam–sliced, skinless, chicken breast; potatoes; salt; grated-butternut squash; sugar; pomegranate paste; Persian rice; kosher butter; walnuts; nutmeg; cinnamon; molasses

Tamarind Fish–bass filets; tamarind paste; pomegranate; white onions; olive oil; dill; garlic; almonds; barberry paste; saffron; pepper; lemon juice; turmeric; sesame; apricots

Home-made Persian ice cream–rose water; saffron; carrot juice; egg yokes; Persian sugar; vanilla; heavy Kosher cream; lemons; almonds; pistachios.

Missy, wearing a short azure frock, eagerly scribbled down the recipes on a yellow, lined pad taken from her brown leather purse. She is copied down to the timing and heat directions, the ingredient proportions.

"Awesome, Mme. Castellane!" our teenage heroine repeated. "Wonderful! Maybe you should consider opening a restaurant?"

"You are an excellent cook, Mme. Castellane. Your interpretation of each dish is exquisite!" added Sister Claire, The British nun's Iranian Auntie made her niece no stranger to fine Persian cuisine.

"Yes, my Véronique is quite an accomplished, such a multifaceted lady!" observed Richard of his blood-sister with rightful pride.

Firebird smiled demurely, made a graceful curtsey.

"I deeply regret never having met Pascale," lamented *Missy*. "Geographically, she and I actually lived close together. We were forever in just walking distance. Only stupid men's politics kept us apart during Pascale's lifetime."

"I much regret it as well, Cherie," replied Firebird, shaking a dash of nutmeg into the simmering pot. "Madame is confident you two little girls would instantly have become the fastest of friends–become the closest–the most loyal of idealistic, junior buddies."

Firebird next added graded squash to the bubbling mix on the stove.

"I am sure," she said, "you special chums would have also enjoyed making this particular stew. I am sure you two girls would become the greatest little chefs around."

"Yes, surely we would, Mme. Castellane," concurred *Missy*.

"Well, in another worldly way, the kids' meeting can still be achieved," encouraged Sister Genevieve. "Now that *Missy* is selected to become the leader of our cause–*Pascale's cause*–the two Dears can be united at last."

"They are becoming united in history!" proclaimed Duchess de Charpentier. This five Olympic track gold medalist was clad tonight all in white. Her body conveyed a timeless, delicate, vulnerable fragrance.

"Yes, indeed, my Rose dearest!" answered Firebird. Suppose the nimble footed Duchess de Charpentier was named Marie-Adrienne-Julienne-Michele-Raymonde de Valois, her best friend since childhood always called her soul-mate *Rose*. Setting down a soup spoon being used to stir a third large pot, the prima ballerina clapped enthusiastically, all the other adults in the dining hall soon joining in. "Yes, Rose honey, yes, my friends. Henceforth, the two little girls will be joined forever in history!"

Missy accepted her admirers' praise with a humble bow, her eyes set toward the floor.

If any element of uncertainty once lurked in the back of this adolescent's mind as to what role adults expected *Missy* to assume, that nagging doubt existed no more.

I

"We ought to watch to the television now," Firebird instructed her friends after the feast was memorably complete. "I was told earlier that Markovsky is going to deliver an important announcement to the nation. We had better listen."

She employed a remote control gadget to turn on a color television placed atop a mahogany lowboy with lace coverlet and shined brass shelf handles. Her guests gathered around to listen. Addressing his audience from across the TV screen, the President spoke in a worried, rattled tone of voice. He exhibited harried, shameful comportment in his body. The listeners in the parish house immediately knew they would not like what they were about to hear.

"As President of the French Republic–being fully cognizant of my responsibility both to preserve the liberty of my fellow citizens and to serve as commander of the armed forces–"

"I already don't care for the sound of this rat's harangue!" said Sister Claire.

"Nor do I!" added Sister Genevieve.

"–having scrupulously considered the military's quite legitimate grievances and its most useful proposals on how to correct them–I believe it is my obligation to–"

"This does not sound good at all!" injected Duchess de Charpentier, taking her precious twins close.

"I'm of the same opinion, Rose" was the comment of Firebird.

"I therefore, instruct the police to temporarily detain the following–"

"The weasel is giving in to the military!" all at the table cried.

As if in a single motion, they all, each, turned to Rolande de Montfort.

All eyes looked yearningly to her to receive the answer.

"Well," mused the youngest member of a historic clan of courtesan kingmakers, "If my friends leave me no choice but to become their leader, if they give me no alternative than to become the new *Little Marie,* I guess I'll become the new *Little Marie!*"

"The scoundrel! The traitor!" exclaimed Rolande, slipping easier than she ever dared imagine into her appointed role."Markovsky is abandoning us, the ungrateful pig!"

Duchess de Charpentier, age thirty-three, being closest to her at the table, Celine's *Treasure* took the peeress's right adult hand in both protective teenage own.

"What should we do, Rolande dear?" humbly pleaded the five-time Olympic gold medalist. Once, a grand dame seeming just stepped from a Gordon Parks photograph in *Vogue,* she once as commanding a figure as history ever produced, Pascale Kedari's beloved **Mistress,** Europe's **La Duchesse** never recovered her original fine health or bold spirit after her protegee's brutal death. "What should we do next, dear?

"First of all, Your Grace," answered Rolande, "we must all get out of here!"

As if in fulfillment of a prophesy, trucks carrying heavily armed troops now parked just outside the parish house. A few moments later, loud, agitated knocks sounded at the apartment's front oak door.

"Let us in! Let us in!" demanded soldiers in hoarse, angry voices. "Let us in in the name of the law! In the name of the French Republic!"

"I will stay here," quickly volunteered Father Richard. "I don't believe they will immediately nab a priest. I will think of some nonsense to detain them with while you ladies get out the back way!"

Patter

Patter

Patter

Further anxious feminine patter

Swift down a musty, dark, creaking, back stairway, the five women and two children rushed; they temporarily removed their high heels to hasten the anxious trek.

"It must have felt something like this for the Jews when they were fleeing the Collaborators!" thought Rolande as she hurriedly led her companions: first, down the staircase; next: out across the dim-lit church close; finally: into the narrow street. If not a repeat of the Holocaust, the present situation certainly evoked legitimate reminders.

Polaris

"WHERE HAVE THEY ALL gone? Where have they all gone!" cried Duchess Raymonde de Charpentier in an anxious voice. "I thought all the university students and labor militants would quickly come out to support us! Instead, they are nowhere to be found! Are they going to take the coup passively?"

And so, it thus initially appeared. The narrow, serpentine, cobblestone paths of the Medieval *Latin Quarter* were dark, silent, empty. News of the attempt at a military takeover already spread, it nevertheless looked as if the reliably rambunctious inhabitants of the 5th Arrondissement had suddenly lost their nerve. The shutters of all the closely-packed, similar, four and five story limestone buildings running parallel each side of the winding streets were shut tight, the thick oak front doors sealed. No slivers of anemic light emanated from cracks or slits to indicate inhabitants cringed behind house walls. Street lamps unlit and bulbs in shops and restaurants switched off completed this environment of unwelcoming, soupy blackness.

"Help! Help! I'm scared! I'm scared!" cried Duchesse de Charpentier in panic. She felt abandoned in the impenetrable night.

"No! No! We're here for you. Mama" pleaded the twins: Marie-Delphine and Marie-Albertine, they holding their frightened stepmother tight. "Don't be frightened Mama. We're both here to protect you! We'll never leave you, Mama!"

"And where is Véronique?" shouted Duchess de Charpentier.

"Where is Véronique?"

'Don't worry, Rose! I am right here for you and the twins!" answered Firebird, clutching both mother and twins, she trying to project a responsible, comforting manner. "Maybe the twins and I can't see you, Rose, but we're still here to protect you."

"Have we been abandoned?" asked Sister Claire's anxious disembodied voice, her usual allies in the neighborhood seeming to have fled.

"Are we deserted?" questioned Sister Genevieve, her words too seeming those of a formless spirit traveling the ether.

Amidst such dense night, the seven companions were unable to perceive they all stood just steps apart. Only the click of their high heels on ancient cobblestones indicated the women and girls dwelt even on the same planet.

"Let's not lose our heads," encouraged Rolande, her words too emanating from a bodiless shapeless phantom in the pitch night. "The people may still come out for us! They might have just gone elsewhere. They may be expecting us elsewhere."

"So it could be! So it could be!" replied Duchess de Charpentier, tone of her voice representing cherished hope more than firm conviction.

"But where! Where could our supporters have gone?" asked Firebird.

"They might be found more in the center of the city," answered Rolande.

"Yes! Yes! In the center of the city!" cried the others in disembodied unison.

"But how can we possibly get there?" soon they queried, again invisible.

"Let me investigate," interjected Rolande, taking command. "When I was a kid, Mama sent me to Roman Catholic summer camp in Brittany. I became instantly captivated there by the night sky. I recall Sister Ernestine one of the instructors taught me how to identify what I discovered. Sister Ernestine taught me how to guide myself by the stars like the Phoenicians, like the Greeks, like the Arabs and the Norsemen. We are not in the countryside now, but I still think I can direct us."

She cast her eyes up.

Despite the narrow, serpentine Medieval streets and compact limestone buildings running each side closely parallel, a section of the universe was still visible above Paris. Normally, city light blocks out all planets and constellations. Yet, with this obstruction temporarily removed, the situation was quite different. For the first time in living memory, heavens fascinating humanity since the ancients were again boldly apparent. *Mercury, Venus, Mars, Jupiter, Saturn, Uranus, Neptune; Taurus, Andromeda, Cetus, Leo, Pegasus, Ursa Major, Ursa Minor, Cepheus, Lyra, Perseus, Gemini, Draco, Hydrus, Lynx, Hercules, Scorpius, Corona Borealis, Delphinus, Mensa, Virgo, Bootes, Cassiopeia, Sagittarius, Cancer, Horologium, Cygnus, Orion, The Big Dipper, Pleiades*

"Awesome!" mused Rolande, gazing up at the vivid spectacle. "No, *Very Awesome*! This must be the same night sky that Aeschylus, Caesar, Virgil, and Jesus looked upon! That Eleanor of Aquitaine, Dante, Copernicus, and Shakespeare recognized! These are the same stars and planets that steered Columbus and Magellan, Sir Francis Drake and Captain Cook!"

As she spoke, the girl felt indescribable if no less real communion with history.

Only her mysterious summons on the Embankment was more glorious.

She began to hum Beethoven's 9th. Symphony.

Time passed.

"Mademoiselle Rolande! Mademoiselle Rolande!" cautiously pleaded her companions. "How do we find our way?"

Shaken from her reverie, the young philosopher returned to earth.

"Now follow me," instructed Rolande, at last sensing the presence of the other ladies nearby. "Hold on to me tight and take my lead. But never, never let me go, or you'll be swift lost!"

Missy felt like Ariadne helping Theseus through the Labyrinth.

"Yes, Mademoiselle Rolande! Yes, Mademoiselle Rolande!" responded the other ladies, each one reaching out to firmly grasp their young leader's dress, torso, or upper limbs. "We promise never to let you go, Mademoiselle Rolande!"

Missy imagined herself as Orpheus seeking to bring Eurydice back from Hades.

"Now, don't ever look back, sweethearts!" she warned, remembering the conclusion of that famous myth. "Don't ever look back, or I've lost you forever."

"We promise never to look back, Mademoiselle Rolande."

Understanding the Medieval cobblestone street was narrow, and a parallel wall must be just paced away in either direction, the new Ariadne/Orpheus led her retinue carefully forward

Step

Step

Step

Cautious, exploratory step

"There!" cried Rolande, at last setting her hands upon a house wall.

"*There!*" repeated the loyal others, each one firmly clutching her leader's dress, torso or upper limbs. In this soupy darkness where one might walk in a circle for hours without being aware, touching, if not yet seeing a wall, made hearts leap with joy. If still lost, the travelers knew they now at least wandered in a circumscribed environment.

Rolande again gazed up.

As if she have now become Sinbad the Sailor.

The bold commander searched for the brightest star in the heavens.

It was to be located in the constellation Ursa Minor.

"There! There! There it is!" she cried.

Polaris

The North or Polar Star

"Polaris!" said Rolande, under her breath. "Follow Polaris!"

She now felt as if Odysseus. Despite all the obstacles whimsical fate and the angry gods could place in his way, the king of Ithica still finally reached home.

"Now I know we can make our way!" she assured her retinue, still clutching their leader's dress, torso, or upper limbs. "Once I've found Polaris, I can determine directions. I can locate both where we are at present and where we should go next."

Yes, mademoiselle Rolande! Yes, Mademoiselle Rolande."

"Come with me, girls!" instructed their leader. "Come forward with me. Keep together, girls. Each of you, keep one hand on me and the other on the wall."

Step

Step

Step

Increasing confident but still exploratory-step

"Polaris!" whispered Rolande. "I must keep my eyes on Polaris!"

Seven pairs of feminine hands also ran the thick, solid, Medieval wall.

Touch

Touch

Touch

More steady touch

Difficult to navigate in broad daylight, such narrow, winding, Medieval streets were near impossible to delineate in the night's soupy blackness. Not intimidated, however, Rolande and her loyal disciples pressed on.

"Polaris!" called Rolande, eyes to the obsidian color-sky. "Polaris!"

Step

Step

Step

"Watch out, girls!" Instructed Roland.

"Here comes a space down!"

"Yes, Mademoiselle Rolande! Yes, Mademoiselle Rolande.

In high heels, aristocratic Duchess de Charpentier briefly stumbled at the street corner, only she to be kept safe on her feet by Firebird coming up protectively just behind.

"Polaris! Polaris!"

Touch

Touch

Touch

This human caterpillar, *Missy* at its lead, steadily advanced.

Forward

Forward

Forward

If the world it traveled was obscured in soupy darkness, the high heel shoes and delicate hands propelling a unique female creature became with each succeeding step and touched bolder in motion, more secure in purpose.

"Polaris! Polaris!"

Up one winding pathway

Down another

Along with a third

Crossing a fourth

"Polaris! Polaris!"

With the young philosopher in the lead, her pensive green eyes fixed on the great star, Rolande and her comrades at last, emerged somewhere from the northern mouth of the labyrinthine 5th Arrondissement. But what next? The attempt at a military takeover leading to the shut-off of all electrical power, *The City of Light,* has now become *The City of Darkness.* Even here, closer to the central metropolis, it was near impossible determining one's precise whereabouts if lacking knowledge of tonight's rarely so discernible heavens. Shops, offices, residential buildings, and restaurants were all closed, their window shades and shutters drawn. No anemic ray from hidden bulbs issued through cracks or slits.

Rolande again gazed into the heavens.

"Polaris!" she cried upon locating the eternal North Star, "Polaris!"

"Alright, girls," instructed Mama's *Treasure*. "Now, keep following me. But never once let me go or look back!"

"Yes, Mademoiselle Rolande! Yes, Mademoiselle Rolande!"

"I suspect our supporters will be collecting around the Place de Hotel de Ville and around the Rue Rivoli" speculated the ladies' leader. "That's where they often congregate."

"But how in all God's creation can we ever possibly get there?" pleaded the other members of the genteel caterpillar. Each, one, she yet clutching her captain's dress, torso, or upper limbs.

Theirs was a reasonable question. With all electrical power from the sidewalks out and no traffic signals glowing, no vehicles with accompanying glare sped the nearby roadway. It was almost impossible for the ladies to realize they were now but paces from the uncharacteristically silent, empty Left Embankment.

Polaris

Polaris

The captain of the caterpillar knew her way, however. "Follow me, girls. Hold on to me, and don't look back."

Yes, Mademoiselle Rolande! Yes, Mademoiselle Rolande!"

Step

Step

Step

"Ah! Here we are, at last, girls!" proclaimed the new Odysseus as seven sets of dainty hands rested upon the stone balustrade overlooking the Seine. "We've reached the left bank of the river! We're definitely on our way!"

"Yes, Mademoiselle Rolande! Yes, Mademoiselle Rolande! We're definitely on our way!" cried in loyal unison the others, they each, still each clutching their guide's dress, torso, or upper limbs.

On other nights, even if rainy or overcast, thousands of vivid, independent spots of ivory-shade light dance merrily atop the waters. Slow and murky in a day, the Seine becomes after sunset an excited, sparkling birthday cake. A tasty treat exuberantly welcoming her countless admirers. Amidst this evening's soupy blackness, though, only the touch of stone balustrade and sensation of nothing save cool air beyond demonstrate a river flows just ahead. At least with Medieval cobblestones now replaced by smooth pavement, ladies in high heels can negotiate the unseen path steadier.

Polaris

Polaris

"Let's now head for the Pont Neuf," instructed Rolande. Judging by the position of the North Star, she knew she must guide her followers first left, before later switching, right. "Follow me, sweethearts! Hold together with one hand on your closest partner just ahead and your other hand running along the balustrade."

Step

Step

Step

Step

At last, the seven comrades (five ladies and the twins) reached the famous stone bridge situated at the eastern tip of the Ile de Cité. Upon crossing the Pont Neuf south to north, the equestrian statue of Henry IV at the span's center currently invisible, they set foot on the Right Embankment. Next, making a right, the party advanced west at a similar ever more assured pace. Suppose the soupy blackness, unnatural silence, showed little evidence of dissolving.In that case, the dainty caterpillar advancing through it gave no indication her confidence was in decline.

Stride

Stride

Stride

Stride

"Cherie?" queried third-in-line Firebird of her leader. "Do you still have the recipes for those Persian dishes my little Pascale so much enjoyed?"

"Yes, I do, Madame Castellane!" answered Rolande. "I've got them in my purse."

"Excellent!"

Stride

Stride

Stride

Stride

Despite the darkness, it was certain the moment of decision fast approached.

An unexpected bolt of unnerving dread now shot through Rolande's entire mind and body.

She stumbled, bit her lip, became paralyzed with anxiety.

"Oh, my Lord!" she thought. "Am I truly up to it? Can I really become the next Pascale, become the next *Little Marie*?"

"Fear not, Cherie," intervened second-in-line Sister Claire in a comforting, maternal voice, some of her original dynamism returning. She, like every good Mama, swift read the girl's worried mind. "I know you can do it, Cherie! I am confident you will know precisely what to say and what to do when the moment comes! Remember, even the saints experienced doubt. We are all sure you are the next Pascale!"

"I pray by all that's holy it may be so!" answered Rolande,

"Yes, it will be so, Child!" promised Sister Claire, again she reading the girl's troubled mind. "Yes, child, you will succeed!"

"*Be not overcome by evil,*" silently quoted Rolande from **ROMANS**, "*but overcome evil with good.*"

"*The world is a closed door, a barrier,*" she whispered the words of Simone Weil, "*yet it is also the way through.*"

"Don't fear, Cherie," counseled Sister Claire. Pressing Rolande's shoulders comforting, maternal, she read both the girl's mind, and understood the significance of the famous quotations *Missy* used to fortify herself. "Don't worry, Child, your victory is near!"

"Bless you, Sister Claire!" answered Rolande, tears of gratitude now running her teenage green eyes. "Bless you."

"Now forward, Child," urged the social activist nun, pressing the girl's hand comforting, maternal. "Now forward, Child, lead us as I know you can!"

The momentary pang of doubt overcome, Rolande now strengthened both in heart and soul, marched on to her encounter with history.

Pharoah And All His Chariots

THE SEVEN LADIES AT last reached the broad, extensive Place Hotel de Ville in the 4th Arrondissement. It, during earlier ages, called the Place de Greve, a site where gruesome executions amidst crowds baying for blood were regularly performed. Before sunset, Rolande crossed this same area north to south. At that time, boisterous crowds jammed the historic square. On a huge television screen, football fans were gleefully observing their country's triumph over Germany in the concluding match of the *World Cup*. Now, just hours later, following the outbreak of the worst political crisis in France since Algiers and President Markovsky's disgraceful reaction to it, the once packed and joyful vicinity was left bare and lonely. The large, gold, gray, and off-white, turreted, Renaissance-style municipal office building giving the square its name was too, currently covered in silent, empty darkness.

"Where are they?" exclaimed Sister Claire, casting her eyes in all directions. "Where did our supporters go?"

"Are we again abandoned!" cried Sister Genevieve.

"Don't be concerned," assured Rolande. "All we need to do is show our presence, and the people will then come!

As if by affirmation, several windows in the Hotel de Ville now switched on.

Vivid, living shafts of ivory color light at pierced the soupy darkness.

Rolande and her companions were boldly illuminated in the grounds below.

To those of a spiritual mind, this glow was an endorsement from on high.

The seven each crossed herself.

Then, before the women could adjust their eyes to this sudden radiant glow, the great building's front portal opened, and Brigadier

Aslan appeared. "Over here, ladies!" he beckoned. "Come over here and have Mademoiselle Rolande speak from the balcony!"

"Just in case a crisis of this kind ever occurred, the Hotel de Ville was provided its own power generator," explained Brigadier Aslan. "Nevertheless, I did not want to turn the mechanism on until Mademoiselle Rolande and her friends arrived."

"Yes, Brigadier, you did exactly the right thing," confirmed Rolande, again taking up her role as the team's bold, empathetic leader.

"Indeed, speak from the balcony, Dear," urged Sister Claire, she infected with her commander's optimism.

"So the child should, so the child must!" cried Ashraf Kermanshani, also touched by her young friend's sense of determination.

"Yes, when the people learn that you've come here, Sweetheart," promised Firebird catching the same fever, "I know they will come."

"So they will, so they will!" eagerly added Sister Genevieve, she moments later so dejected.

As if in confirmation, the sound was soon heard of numerous approaching feet, the echo of mounting voices.

"You children go along ahead and look after Mademoiselle Rolande" instructed Duchess de Charpentier to the twins Marie-Delphine and Marie-Albertine. Usually, the little pair were away at boarding school. They were placed under Mother Madeline's kind, erudite supervision at the Duchess's former convent in Normandy. Just by chance did the military coup break out while the girls were home on vacation.

Patter

Patter

Patter

Still more adolescent feminine patter

Advancing ahead of the adults, Rolande and the twins scurried through the elegantly decorated public rooms of the Hotel de Ville's first floor. With their–dark stained panel flooring beneath sumptuous multicolor patterned rugs; cloth-of gold wallpaper; gilded furniture; fine Gobelin tapestries; huge gold-framed mirrors; ornate crystal chandeliers; portraits of noted Parisian artists and statesmen; Rodin statues; Puvis de Chevannes and Morot frescoes looking down from high ceilings–these salons in normal times would instantly summon visitors to long contemplation. On this occasion, however, the newcomers simply sped along the famous halls and up the sweeping marble staircase leading to the balcony on the floor above.

"Now is your moment! Now is your moment!" thought Rolande as she stepped out upon the balcony looking out over the wide Place Hotel de Ville. "Now is the moment to prove that you are worthy of representing Pascale Kedari and all her followers."

By the time Rolande appeared, word of the girl's arrival had so swift and far spread that the great square beneath was filled with a multitude of ardent supporters–men and women, old and young, white, black, oriental, Christian, Jewish, Muslim, all other faiths. Despite the soupy darkness, the immense crowd was made evident not simply through its frequent cheers but also by the abundance of undulating flashlights, glittering smart-phones, and tinkling camera flashes emanating from all directions. It was a site certain to make every speechifier since Pericles pause, doubtful.

"What should I say to them?" pondered Rolande. "I'm no orator."

"Don't worry, Mademoiselle de Montfort," assured the twins, each one reading her older friend's mind. "There is no need for you to be an *orator*–simply say what you feel, what's in your heart."

"Well then," sighed Rolande fatalistically, "here goes."

"Yes," assured the twins, each one in a Catholic schoolgirl uniform, each one pulling up her socks. "Yes, here goes!"

"People," began Rolande, first uneasily but then with increasing confidence. "Ladies, gentlemen. Sisters, brothers, I've been chosen by the *Five Good Ladies*–Sister Claire, Sister Genevieve, Madame Castellane, Duchess de Charpentier, and Professor Eisenberg as the new spokesman of our cause–Pascale Kedari, *Little Marie's* cause. I, therefore, come here tonight in order to say as *Little Marie* would tell you, that we must unite. We must now unite in order to stop the military from taking over. We must now unite in order to stop President Markovsky from shamelessly betraying our democratic republic. Remember, when standing together, the supporters of freedom, the followers of *Little Marie* can never fail in their sense of duty and call to purpose!"

"Not quite silver-tongued oratory," evaluated Rolande. "Cicero and Demosthenes, Aneurin Bevan and Martin Luther King have no fear discovering a rival in me. Still, my words will do."

"So they will, so they will!" encouraged the twins, each in a Catholic schoolgirl uniform, each one pulling up her socks.

On the far side of the square was another of the public murals crafted by Pascale Kedari. This masterpiece, was created not long before her assassination. If currently obscured by night's blackness, the fresco and its teenage artist were also present at this hour. All understood Pascale looked on attentive from another world. Another world, both forever distant and enticingly near.

"I know that standing up to the forces of reaction is precisely what our *Little Marie* would want" "continued Rolande. "I know–*you know*–that is exactly what our *Little Marie is* expecting us to do now!"

The populace roared in approval.

Countless feet stamped agreement.

A constellation of flashlights undulated favorable.

Numberless smart phones and cameras glittered, tinkled endorsement.

Sister Claire, Duchess de Charpentier, and the other ladies from whom Rolande and the twins had rushed ahead were by now too assembled on the balcony.

"Let us each and all demonstrate ourselves to be worthy of Pascale Kedari, our fallen leader!" Rolande declared, the light emanating from within the building out upon the balcony providing a magical, beckoning aspect to both the speaker's body and her evermore commanding words.

"How shall we do it!" Rolande queried, "when we are without weapons?

"Yet no matter!" she told the assembled crowd below. "It's still firmly in our power to bring this about."

"So it is!" responded the entranced listeners. "So it is!"

"Let's turn everything off!" cried Rolande. "Let's shut down the country. Not just here in Paris but across the entire country!"

So we will" thundered the answer. "So we will!"

"You will make *Little Marie* so rightly proud of you," promised Rolande. "Have no doubt of that. *Little Marie* is looking down on us just as I speak."

"So we will make *Little Marie* rightly proud of us! So we can make *Little Marie* so rightly proud of us!"

On hearing Rolande's words, Firebird and Duchess de Charpentier, both standing behind her atop the balcony, each pressed the girl's shoulders tender. "Yes, Sweetheart," they said fondly. "You will certainly make our *Little Marie* view you with love."

The crowd immediately went to work. Not simply those standing in the Place Hotel de Ville joined the effort but soon too, women and men from across the wide metropolis. Not restricted to the nation's capital, the peaceful protest swiftly expanded outward until it encompassing well over half of all France. As word of Rolande's call to action spread in less than an hour, all electrical power from Strasbourg in the east to Nantes in the west, from Toulouse the south to Lille in the north shut off. From Alsace-Lorraine to the tip of Brittany, from Aquitaine to Flanders, a modern, industrialized nation forever dependent on ready access to cheap energy, came to a screeching halt.

Railroads ground to a stop. Office and residential buildings, theaters, cinemas, museums, boulevards, monuments, restaurants, stadiums, and traffic posts all went dark. Lights critical for illuminating major harbors, to guiding pilots into and out of airports, necessary in directing drivers along busy highways and congested avenues, for aiding passage over bridges, through tunnels and canals all went abruptly, dead. Factories idled. Shops closed. Universities recessed. Power plants went quiet. Sports events froze in place. Amidst the sudden darkness, the streets of cities, medium-sized towns, and hamlets all became hopelessly clogged with vehicles. Frantic honking waled in paralyzed, impotent fear. Those attempting to make their way by foot soon discovered they walked in circles without the slightest knowledge of their predicament. Other inhabitants became stranded inside metros caught between stations or elevators stuck between floors. Stock-trading on the Bourse halted.

All in-coming and out-going road and river commerce along the German border, traversing the Lowlands and crossing the Pyrenees, stopped. Barges collided; trucks went off the road; long, serpentine lines of cars jammed bumper to bumper. Along the Atlantic Ocean, English Channel and Bay of Biscay, freighters and cruise ships preparing to dock at the port were suddenly ordered back to sea. At airfields, scores of jetliners were hastily diverted to landing grounds in other countries. Throughout the entire region: cellphone towers malfunctioned; computer, television, radio, and telephone communication went out. It is late September, loss of AC was not as uncomfortable as it would be were this crisis occurring in the summertime.

Fast-paced, contemporary, high-tech France was returned to the wind-drawn, horse-propelled, candle-lit eighteenth century in just minutes.

To the East, in the Rhineland, the military coup plotters developed second thoughts. If General Marchand his fellow conspirators were still in a position to capture Paris, they originally expected launching just a limited, surgical strike. One, in which the defenders of "law and order" swiftly nabbed Rolande and the *Five Good Ladies,* then returned to base without encountering any civilian resistance. However, the massive social protest in Rolande's favor demonstrated any move the army attempted would be met with widespread, united and very active opposition.

Just as the generals began faltering in resolution, so too, their troops experienced grave doubts. Jean and Paul, for instance, who abducted dissident Ashraf off the street, now realized any further military advance might easily involve an attack on their own families, own loved ones. Confronted with such unexpected and concerted vehemence, the army commanders called off the plot. They speedily returned to base and pledged their solid support for the current elected government. As for Markovsky, totally compromised by his cowardly involvement in the scheme, he fled the country.

The insurrection was stopped, democracy was preserved. It was achieved without a single shot being fired, life lost, or soul injured.

"We've done it! We've done it!" cried Rolande, long red hair in her pretty face like Pascale. "We defeated the forces of reaction! We proved that no matter how powerful the armies and bankers and industrialists think they are, ultimately, it's the people who decide things in this country!" Waving her fist in the air triumphant, she next cast off her heels so she might better jump up-and-down. "We, the people, won! And we won decisively!"

"Isn't the child a darling?" mused Duchess de Charpentier to Véronique.

"So, the child is, Rose!" answered Firebird.

"Indeed, Mademoiselle de Montfort is our cherished dear!" exclaimed the crowd.

"France is saved!" proclaimed all.

Mademoiselle de Montfort looked away demure, curtseyed deep.

Sister Claire sprinkled her with blue, white, and red roses.

Once again, the girl felt the presence of the Holy Spirit. It was a force as powerful as it was also invisible, as clear as it was too, unseen "Thank you," Rolande prayed in confirmation. "Thank you for making me your instrument. Thank you for making me an instrument of your everlasting glory."

Across the way, *Little Marie* gestured warm approval from her mural.

The nation and economy took a bit longer turning back on after first summarily shut off. However, this delay was much sweetened for the populace by the sudden, incontestable knowledge ordinary men and women received of their power to shape larger, historical events.

Release

THE HEAVY, IRON CELL door suddenly creaked open.

A bright shaft of ivory-color light knifed through the musty, humid darkness.

Startled, two-foot rats scurried into the dank shadows.

Frightened, thumb-length roaches raced the grimy, chipped walls.

"Madame Celine, Madame Celine!" cried Brigadier Aslan, entering the dungeon. "I've come to take you home now."

"Brigadier Aslan? Is that you?" replied the *Good Little Soldier* plaintive, she curled into a ball, shielding her eyes from the burst of light to which she was as yet unaccustomed. "Is that you, my commander?"

"Yes indeed, Sweetheart, it's actually your commander!" promised the French-Turkish spy chief. "I've come to take you and your friends Madame Ashraf and Madame Matilda out of this filthy, dreary, godforsaken place. I've come to bring you girls home."

"Is it really-really all over, Brigadier Aslan?" asked the *Good Little Soldie*r, words unsure, her body still curled into a ball, yet shielding her eyes from the burst of light to which she was as unaccustomed. "Is this awful nightmare reallyfinally over?"

"Yes, Indeed, it's all over!" assured Brigadier Aslan. "Your–**our**–nightmare is now over."

"How did it happen? And so quick! Only minutes ago, I told my Ashraf and my Matilda that we three might be trapped in this ghastly hole for possibly years. I was teaching my two dears to prepare themselves–to be brave as they underwent so much pain and suffering."

"Well, no need to worry or steel-yourself anymore, Sweetheart," guaranteed Brigadier Aslan. "You and your girls are free to come home now!"

"As for the reason why our resolution and our deliverance happened so fast," the old warrior continued, "It was principally due to how the ladies performed."

"The ladies?"

"Quite so! Especially your younger daughter and her new friends at the church."

"See! See! See! I said it would be so!" piped Celine to her cellmates proudly. "I said it would be so, my Ashraf, my Matilda! Remember just as at the fall of Singapore, the ladies stepped forward and were heroic. The ladies set a glorious example for all the men to follow!"

She paused to catch a delighted breath.

"But please, commander, tell me more! Please tell me more!"

"It was especially thanks to your daughter Rolande" explained Brigadier Aslan. "She rallied all the people to launch a nationwide protest against Markovsky and the army. She and her followers closed down more than half of France. The army plotters lost heart and surrendered. Markovsky fled the country. Democracy is preserved. And all took place because of your younger daughter. She was so brave. She was so magnificent. The nation owes her so much. Sister Claire Preston sprinkled her with flowers as they do in honor of *Little Marie.*"

"Well, it's only natural, I guess," remarked the *Good Little Soldier.* "After all, Treasure possesses all my own best genes and DNA!"

She again paused, reflective, as her eyes grew accustomed to the new light. Next, she kissed maternally, hugged tenderly, her other two loyal daughters: Ashraf Kermanshani and Matilda Eisenberg.

Then, like Sir Alec Guinness emerging from the sweat-box in *The Bridge on the River Kwai,* Celine de Montfort came out of the prison cell haggard, exhausted, but she no less confident in the ultimate righteousness of her cause. "Yes, it's just as I expected. After all, I bore the child. This is the way I raised the child. It's how I taught the child to conduct herself. It's all just as I should have assumed all along."

"Come, Sweetheart!" insisted Brigadier Aslan, offering the *Good Little Soldier* his arm. "I will take you–escort the proud Mama home. She and her brood have not eaten in several days. It's also high-time Mama practiced her piano."

Ladies Should Not Be Vindictive

FOLLOWING THE OVERTHROW OF the Markovsky regime, France has entered a long period of peace and prosperity. One-strengthened through her citizens' consciousness of their mutual responsibility for maintaining the blessings of this new era.

In seeming divine affirmation, the brilliant frescoes of *Little Marie*, they recently subject to the government's not-so benevolent neglect, again became the open pride and joy of Paris and many other French cities. Local inhabitants again freely hold the magical girl's creations to their hearts and eagerly display her art to visitors worldwide.

No heavy retribution was brought upon the coup plotters. Instead, General Marchand and the other military chiefs were permitted to take a gracious early retirement, handing the armed forces over to *Marshal* Aslan. Provided he agreed to never return to France and keep a low profile, former President Markovsky was told Paris would not seek his extradition or put him on trial. Why were he and the other schemers treated so leniently? As Countess de Montfort often insisted: "Ladies should not be vindictive."

In the coming years, the *Good Ladies* kept *Little Marie's* message alive when few would listen and fewer still follow its teaching. Each achieved her just reward and degree of historical recognition.

Professor Matilda Eisenberg, the first in the group to encounter Pascale Kedari, during she and the teenager's accidental meeting on the airplane flight between Frankfurt and Paris, served for several years as Minister of National Education. During her term of office, *Brendel's Daughter* instituted the most significant and most far-reaching educational reforms in French history. After leaving office, Matilda became the much celebrated director of the University of Paris.

Appointed by Professor Eisenberg as leader of the Mathematics Department was Ashraf Kermanshani/Mrs. Villers. In her new position, this Iranian-American at last acquired wide cognition of her intellectual talents. With each new paper she publishes and class she teaches, Ashraf proves to the world yet again that girls *are* good at math.

Sister Claire Preston and her chum Sister Genevieve Fauré continue to actively promote their religious order's message of all embracing, all inclusive social improvement. If yet denied entrance into the United States by the *McCarran-Walter Act,* the nuns receive well-earned admiration for their many good deeds elsewhere in the world. On regular occasions returning to Paris, the two are always eager to give flower-bearing visitors a guided tour of the beloved *New Arena Chapel.* If the traditionalist from No. 3 Rue Artemis is among the pilgrims, both nuns make sure to give their tour while wearing a habit.

Véronique Castellane rediscovered the ability that made her, until age twenty-six, the greatest prima ballerina of the century. If she could not again become the original Firebird after years of semi-retirement, Véronique was still young enough and insufficient practice to once more win the admiration of both critics and fans across the planet.

Duchess Raymonde de Charpentier also recovered much of her former dynamism. Once more, she appears as an aristocratic figure stepped from a Gordon Parks photograph in *Vogue,* La Duchesse is once again the ambassador for *UNICEF* and a highly successful international diplomatic troubleshooter.

To celebrate the dawning of this new era, Celine performed yet another televised concert. This evening, she is wearing a white, strapless opera gown, her magical fingers played a no less memorable rendition of Concerto no. 5. in E-flat Major by Beethoven; Concerto no. 1 in E-Minor by Chopin; Concerto no. 1 opus 35 by Shostakovich; Concerto in A-Minor op. 54 by Schumann; and Concerto no. 1 in A-Minor op. 14 by Grieg. As usual, *CD*s of Celine's newest performance was soon easily available on *AMAZON,* at other popular outlets or in pirated version from China, Vietnam, Thailand and South Korea.

To complete the happy change of affairs, Ashraf Kermanshani persuaded her sister Golbihar to come to France and offer the public a series of displays of her own superb Olympic figure skating skill. Especially, Golbihar's unprecedented quadruple aerial twirl, or: *Kermanshani Move.*

And what of the *Montfort Ladies*? Having exerted such wide indirect power over European society for more than five centuries, did their ability continuing to delicately shape human events evaporate with the new era? Far from it. "A woman's work is never done!" sighs Celine. If long associated in the popular mind with the conservative status quo, this clan depicted by painters from Michelangelo to David Hockney sees themselves rather as the defenders of peace and stability. Once President Markovsky and the Right attempted ruling without the ladies' mediating influence, the noble dames shifted their critical influence elsewhere. The newly ascendant left, remembering its fate the last time it tried governing without the countesses' oversight, thought better of it this time and consented to the Montforts' discreet chaperoning. If as usual remaining in the shadows, the residents of No. 3. Rue Artemis exercise no small part in assuring this new era remains one of progress and good feeling. "Government is the men's department," Celine so often insists. "Rough-and-tumble politics is no place for weak women. Still, that does not mean we in skirts cannot occasionally offer moral support from the sidelines."

I

A few weeks later, the Australian polymath's Faithful Little Mate was christened in St. G Church. Father Richard performed the ceremony as *The Five Good Ladies* and their intimates looked on.

"See, Cherie! See!" piped Countess de Montfort to her younger daughter with all rightful maternal pride. "Didn't Mama tell you she would get Mrs. Villers baptized before the onset of winter!"

"So you did, Mama," answered Rolande with a smile. "I confess I had my doubts about your chance of success, but you never faltered in resolution."

"Amen! The Virgin be praised! Another lost sheep is returned to the flock."

"So indeed, Mama. You've returned another lost sheep to the flock! A most important lost sheep, too!"

"I hope I've done the right thing," ventured the new Marie-Isabelle, shyly. If happy at the step she'd taken, her previous strong secularism could not but leave a tad of anxiety. "Before I met you and your lovely friends and family, Celine, I never thought much about religion. I certainly believe I really did the right thing today."

"Of course you've done a splendid thing, Sweetheart!" assured the Countess, bubbling with joy, well-earned satisfaction.

She applied this newest member of the Roman Catholic Church a warm peck on painted lips, pressed the convert to her bosom.

"I hope Mr. Villers also approves of my decision."

"But of course he approves, Sweetheart!" promised the Countess. "I'm absolutely confident Mr. Villers is looking down happily from Heaven this very instant. He is ever so pleased with the choice of his Faithful Little Mate."

Once more applied this newest member of the Roman Catholic Church a warm peck on painted lips, she pressed the convert to her bosom.

"So, what made you finally decide to take this crucial step, Madame" inquired Sister Genevieve, taking photographs.

Marie-Isabelle pondered for a moment.

She adjusted her chapeau.

Then realized the answer to the question was for a mathematician, unmistakable.

"I concluded that if two women as different and seemingly irreconcilable as me and Countess de Montfort could become the dearest of buddies, a greater force–call it God, call it Christ, the Virgin if you prefer Sister–must wish it so. After receiving the unexpected blessing of Countess de Montfort's priceless love, I understood I had no alternative but to embrace the force which brought our love about."

II

Time passed.

So too, earthly seasons,

The *Missy Collection* is becoming a distinguished research center.

"Mama could happily remain just right *here* on this very spot for the rest of her life," declared Countess de Montfort, her gloved-right forefinger tapping on the stone upon which she and Rolande now sat. The two were contemplating the splendid view of Paris available atop the heights of Montmartre.

"That's certainly a not at all unreasonable desire, Mama." The pretty duo crossed their legs opposite, same. Hem of each one's skirt receding.

Comrades pecked lips warm.

Both, taking the other gloved right hand affectionately tight.

Mother and daughter? Or big and little sister? For observers, it was often difficult to tell.

The two courtesans wore: identical short, designer, sleeveless dresses; the same neutral shade pantyhose; a similar pair of high heels; a comparable necklace, wide-brimmed chapeau.

The body of each noble dame conveyed a delicate, sweet, vulnerable fragrance.

Save for a fleeting pinch of whiteness scattered here and there, and no clouds obstructed the soft, fresh, blue sky.

From the summit of these famous steps–all the multicolored spires, palaces, and battlements; all the wide avenues, parks, and river spans; every great monument, castle, and stately square of Paris–stretched out welcoming, below. Crowds, traffic, and noise: the modern struggle for daily existence, were silent, invisible from these heights. The metropolis appeared as if she is a matchless, enviable maiden. One, radiating her purity in all its forms to a longing, fallen world.

Half-way down the marble staircase, three Algerian youths in western dress, each approximately Rolande's own age, were playing a tune dear to both Celine and her daughter's heart. One boy was at the drums, the two others sitting nearby, accompanied with guitars. A remarkably good performance it was, too! A girl, likely the boys' sister, dressed in jeans, logo-marked pullover sweatshirt, and running shoes traveled along the upper steps passing a basket for contributions. If her brothers wore *Yankees* caps, their sister sported a *Red Sox*. Most visitors idly tossed-in a small coin. However, when the basket reached the summit, Celine and Rolande each opened her *Hermes Birkin* purse and in a show of appreciation for the musicians' fine performance, contributed a mid-size currency note.

"Bless you, Madame!" exclaimed the Algerian girl to Celine upon discovering the unexpected ample size of the contribution. "Bless you, Madame! My brothers and I are most grateful"

She curtseyed to the countess deep, sincere, and humble.

"Bless you too, Mademoiselle!" exclaimed the Algerian girl to Rolande upon she noticing the unusually large amount of the donation. "Bless you too, Mademoiselle! My brothers and I are most grateful to you as well."

She curtseyed to Rolande deep, sincere and humble.

The two courtesans acknowledged the Algerian girl's immense gratitude with winning smiles.

"Bless you and your brothers as well, Child!" replied Celine. "There are no one's songs, my friend and I love to hear more than those of Bob Dylan. You and your brothers perform them so well. You sweethearts deserve a show of respect for such lovely work."

"So indeed, you deserve a show of respect," added Rolande.

"Bless you, bless you both!" again responded the Algerian girl. "May God always look kindly upon and preserve both you great ladies."

III

"Look!"

"Look!"

"Look!"

"Look!"

"Look!"

"Look!"–once more cried some of Countess de Montfort's loyal followers.

"I's our Celine!"

"It's our Celine!"

"It's our Celine!"

"It's our Celine!"

"It's our Celine!"

"It's actually our very own real, live, precious Celine!":

Scramble

Patter

Lunge

Run

Scurry

Frantic charge–as the followers approached.

"Now, now! Don't worry my faithful champions," assured Countess de Montfort, with an endearing smile. Crossing pretty legs opposite, hem of her short, sleeveless, designer dress again receded. "Whenever my protectors come for a visit, I make sure I see to all their concerns."

"Ooh, we! It's really her!"

"Ghee whiz!"

"Golly, wow!"

"The Virgin be praised! Its really her!

"Let me take a picture!"

"Let me take a picture, too!"

"Priceless! Priceless!"

Snap

Snap

Snap

Snap

Snap

Snap, snap, further overjoyed camera snaps.

Sheets of paper, exhibition fliers, postcards, museum pamphlets were all brought forth in a desperate effort so that they might each receive upon them the royal insignia.

"Please!"

"Please!"

"Please!"

"Oh, but of course," promised Countess de Montfort, crossing pretty legs opposite, hem of her short, sleeveless, designer dress again receding. "Of course, I'll give you my autograph." Light from the windows of nearby thousand-year-old St. Pierre Church gave her pantyhose an attractive shine.

Opening her *Hermes Birkin* handbag, Countess de Montfort removed a fountain pen and proceeded to sign all the outstretched documents. Each message she wrote was *Entre Nous* and set down in superb feminine calligraphy.

To: Francoise,
with the memories we can treasure a lifetime and beyond.
From: your Celine

To: Marie-Agnes,
whom I hold dear now and always.
From: her special buddy, Celine

To: Marie-Claudette,
who is every day in my thoughts and prayers.
From: her pal, Celine

To: Julie,
who lives in my heart and shares my soul.
From: your trusty Celine

To: Edmonde:
without whose love I could never live.
From: her gentle Celine

To: Minette:
my protector and my queen,
From: her ever- loyal subject Celine's

After signing all the proffered requests, Celine glanced at her watch.

It was a delicate timepiece on a delicate wrist.

"We must go now, Sweetheart," she remarked to Rolande upon observing the hour. "Mama must take you to the opening of your new show. Besides the press, National Education Minister Madame Eisenberg has also graciously consented to be there. It should be quite an event!"

"I'd be honored if you accompany my daughter and me," suggested Countess de Montfort to her latest army of admirers. "In about sixty minutes, *The Missy Collection* is scheduled to open its latest show to the public. I know you will each find the exhibits fascinating."

"Make sure to keep an eagle eye on her," Mama advised the crowd, casting a warning, protective, satisfied look at Rolande. "My daughter– my Treasure–is going to become the greatest *Montfort Lady* of them all!"